ALSO BY LAURA SHOVAN

The Last Fifth Grade of Emerson Elementary

WENDY
L A M B
BOOKS

Text copyright © 2018 by Laura Shovan
Jacket art copyright © 2018 by Kevin Whipple

All rights reserved. Published in the United States by Wendy Lamb Books, an imprint of Random House Children's Books, a division of Penguin Random House LLC, New York. Wendy Lamb Books and the colophon are trademarks of Penguin Random House LLC.

A line from a poem by Joy Harjo, "This Morning I Pray for My Enemies," appears on page 220. This poem is found in *Conflict Resolution for Holy Beings: Poems*, copyright © 2015 by Joy Harjo, published by W. W. Norton & Co., Inc.

Visit us on the Web! rhcbooks.com
Educators and librarians, for a variety of teaching tools, visit us at RHTeachersLibrarians.com

Library of Congress Cataloging-in-Publication Data
Name: Shovan, Laura, author.
Title: Takedown / Laura Shovan.
Description: First edition. | New York : Wendy Lamb Books, [2018] | Summary: Told in separate voices, sixth-graders Mikayla, a wrestler like her brothers, and Lev, part of the Fearsome Threesome, become good wrestling partners and friends, but there can be only one winner at the State competition.
Identifiers: LCCN 2017030357 (print) | LCCN 2017041591 (ebook) | ISBN 978-0-553-52143-6 (ebook) | ISBN 978-0-553-52141-2 (trade) | ISBN 978-0-553-52142-9 (lib. bdg.) | ISBN 978-0-553-52144-3 (pbk.)
Subjects: | CYAC: Wrestling—Fiction. | Competition (Psychology)—Fiction. | Sex role—Fiction. | Friendship—Fiction. | Middle schools—Fiction. | Schools—Fiction. | Family life—Fiction.
Classification: LCC PZ7.1.S51785 (ebook) | LCC PZ7.1.S51785 Tak 2018 (print) | DDC [Fic]—dc23

The text of this book is set in 12-point ScalaPro.
Interior design by Bob Bianchini

Printed in the United States of America

10 9 8 7 6 5 4 3 2 1

First Edition

Random House Children's Books supports the First Amendment and celebrates the right to read.

FOR ROB, MY PARTNER THROUGH IT ALL

CHAPTER 1

Mickey

I have two names. At home, I'm Mikayla. It's the name my mom picked, a gift she gave herself when I turned out to be not the third son Dad wanted, but the daughter of her secret dreams.

Mom chose my name because it sounds like a melody. It starts with a note—*Mi*—and ends with a note—*La*—like that "Do, a Deer" song in her favorite movie, *The Sound of Music.*

My mom is a really good singer. In high school, she was in all the musicals. Now she saves her voice for when we're alone in the car, with no older brothers to complain about her taste in music.

Sometimes I wish Mom didn't like my name so much. She makes everyone call me *Mikayla,* all three syllables. When I was a baby, my brothers thought that was a lot of name for a little person. Evan and Cody tried to call me *Kay-Kay,* but Mom would have none of it.

If Dad had gotten his way, I'd probably have a short name like my brothers. Their names sound like punches,

Evan and Cody, a right hook and a left jab. I was supposed to be the uppercut, to give Dad the full boy combination.

It was Evan who said my name was too soft if I wanted to be a wrestler like my brothers. Four years ago, after our parents split up, Dad put a wrestling mat in his basement so Evan and Cody could train whenever they wanted. I wasn't about to play quietly while they practiced moves with cool names like *whizzer* and *cement mixer*. I was seven years old and full of energy. My best friend Kenna and I were taking dance lessons, but it wasn't enough. I wanted to wrestle.

"What you need is a tough name," Evan said one day. "No one's going to take a wrestler named *Mikayla* seriously."

"They'll take me seriously when they see me take you down," I said, jumping on Evan's back. He was in eighth grade, solid as a tree, and still growing. That was the year Evan won state champ.

"What are you going to do, pirouette for them?" Cody said. My face got hot. I hated when my brothers ganged up on me. They knew I was about to lose it.

"Suck it up," Evan said. "No crying on the mat."

I had to show my brothers I was strong enough to wrestle. Dad was spending every weekend at tournaments with Evan and Cody. They hardly ever took me along. I was tired of staying behind with Mom and not seeing my father. Maybe Dad would let me join a team, if Evan said I was ready.

I grabbed his right leg behind the knee and pulled it hard against my chest. Evan hopped, then wrapped his arms around my middle and lifted me off the ground, breaking my hold.

"Fight fair!" I said.

"Settle down, Kay-Kay," Cody teased.

Evan had my arms wrapped up, so I kicked at Cody. But I was too high off the mat to make contact.

He laughed. "Mick the Kick. *Really* tough."

"Zero percent funny," I said.

Evan loosened his grip. "Not Mick," he said. "That's a boy's name. How about Mickey?"

That's how Mickey became my second name, my second self. Mikayla is for home and for school, where I work hard to stay on the honor roll. School is the one place where I know I can dominate my brothers. But put a wrestling singlet on me, and I'm Mickey Delgado, determined as any boy on the mat. I may not be the strongest kid, but I'm one of the quickest. And my rec league coach says Kenna and I are two of the smartest wrestlers he's ever seen.

Kenna is more than my best friend. She's been my training partner since I started wrestling. Now that we're eleven and in sixth grade, it's the perfect time to join a travel team. We're both good enough to test our skills against competitive wrestlers. Not just from our own state, Maryland, but kids from Pennsylvania, Virginia, and New Jersey too. I hope our new coach is ready, because there's a whole lot of girl power coming his way.

CHAPTER 2

Lev

I am a wrestler
who loves to win,
an animal lover
and walker of dogs,
specifically Grover,
our chubby old beagle.
Sometimes, I pretend
that I do amazing things,
win the Olympic gold medal
in wrestling, get invited
to the White House,
shake the president's hand.
What does the future
hold for me?

My pencil stops moving. Mr. Vanderhoff wants us to finish writing our poems, but I'm stuck. The only future I can think about is wrestling. The season starts next week. This year, I'm making it all the way to States.

"I have big plans for you, sixth graders. As soon as the first quarter concludes, we are beginning a new project. Writing! Creativity! Invention!" Mr. Van says in his booming voice, because he is incapable of talking like a normal person. Still, he's my favorite teacher at Meadowbrook Middle School. "Who wants to read a poem?"

I sit on my hands so I won't be tempted to volunteer. Bryan Hong, my best friend, gives me a sideways look. He's trying not to laugh at me, but I don't see his hand going up.

Emma Peake waves her arm in the air. Marisa Zamora raises hers slowly. Bryan's face turns pink. I'm not supposed to know he likes Marisa, but it's obvious.

Then Nick Spence puts up his hand. He's the only other serious wrestler in our grade. It's Nick's fault I didn't make it to the Maryland state tournament last year. He ruined my chance to qualify. Then he ruined my life at school by telling everyone I cried when he beat me.

We were on the playground. One minute, I was rounding the kickball bases, and the next, kids were asking if it was true that Nick made me cry at a tournament. The girls didn't seem to care. Especially when Emma shrugged and said, "We're humans. Our bodies wouldn't make tears if we weren't supposed to cry."

But the fifth-grade boys did care. Kids who would have taken my side and told Nick to stop being a bully at the beginning of the year, they laughed. A couple of weeks later, I quit playing kickball. Every time I missed a play, the guys would say, "Don't cry, Lev," and rub their eyes pitifully. Bryan stopped playing too. He's that kind of friend.

I'm not going to let it happen again. Half the kids at Meadowbrook Middle don't know me. And the ones who do? I'm going to show them that I'm tougher than Spence, on the mat and off.

Bryan and I roll our eyes at each other when Mr. Van calls on Nick.

Nick stands next to his desk, the way Mr. Van taught us. He's got this weird haircut—shaved on the sides with longer hair on top. He picks up his notebook and tilts his head in Emma Peake's direction. His blond hair flops over to one side.

Not wrestling, I think as Nick opens his mouth to read. *Not wrestling.* I don't want him to accuse me of copying his poem. That would be a Spence thing to do.

"'I Am,'" Nick says, so loud and sure, no one in the room makes a sound.

> I am an eagle who dives at my prey.
> I am an athlete. My body obeys me.
> I want to win, no matter what the prize is.
> When it's time to compete,
> I pretend I have wings.
> I'm above the world,
> watching, waiting for my chance
> to strike.

I don't applaud with the rest of my class. Instead, I slip my wrestling notebook out from under my language arts journal. I always carry the notebook with me. When I need a break at tournaments, or when school gets me down, I find a quiet spot and start sketching or writing.

Mr. Van starts complimenting Spence on his eagle metaphor. Big deal. The Eagles are Nick's wrestling team. Of course he wrote about being an eagle. I tune out and focus on my notebook.

I had him, I write, remembering.

Third period, up by one. I step back, circle, waiting out the clock.
The ref holds up a fist. He knows I'm stalling.
I can't give Nick the point. Coach screams SHOOT!
I grab Nick's leg, pull it in, but instead of spinning,
falling to the ground, he pushes off, rolls like a log on a river,
with me dancing, trying to stay afloat. I twist,
but I'm stuck on my back. His chest covers mine
like a log jamming a river. I still hear the S L A P
when the ref's palm hits the mat.

When the ref raised Nick's arm, I couldn't drag my eyes off the floor. He'd been taunting me the whole tournament. But wrestling is all about leaving it on the mat, so I shook Nick's hand as hard as I could, jogged over to shake his coach's hand, and rushed back to Coach Billy.

"Why'd you tell me to take a shot?" I asked Coach. I was still up by one. A few more seconds and I would have made it to States.

Coach Billy put an arm around my shoulders. "Sometimes you've got to be aggressive, Lev," he said. "You can't always play it safe. Especially in a close match."

I left the school gym and found an empty hallway where I could kick the wall and, yeah, I may have cried a little. But that's how wrestling goes. Some losses are tough. Nick knows that, but he told the guys at school anyway. He and his friends boo-hooed at me for weeks, rubbing their eyes and making ugly frowns.

Bryan and Emma told me to ignore them, but Nick is still my nemesis. I learned that word from my father, who I call Abba, which is Hebrew for "Dad." A nemesis is someone like Lex Luthor, whose only purpose is to destroy Superman and take over the world. Except, in my life, Nick's only purpose is to destroy me and ruin my chance of making the state wrestling championship.

I read over the words in my notebook. Bryan's kicking my foot. I don't look up. He kicks harder, but it's too late. A huge shadow falls across my desk.

"What's grabbed your attention there, Mr. Sofer?" Mr. Van peers down at my notebook.

I look at the board. " 'The Tell-Tale Heart'?" Wrong answer.

When the bell rings, Mr. Van calls me to his desk. "It's not like you to daydream in class, Lev. What's on your mind?"

Before I can get out the word *nothing,* my mouth is saying, "Nick Spence. He's on our rival wrestling team."

"I see," says Mr. Van. "The poet Rumi said, 'Bestow your love, even on your enemies. If you touch their hearts, what do you think will happen?' "

"I can barely shake hands with the guy, Mr. Van. There is no way I'm touching his heart."

Mr. Van loves quoting poetry. Other language arts teachers have posters like *AMAZING ADJECTIVES* on their walls. Mr. Van's ceiling tiles are painted with lines of poetry and book covers. I look up and spot *The Tales of Edgar Allan Poe,* which we've been reading for our horror unit. I shudder, wondering if Nick would be the guy stashing my heart under some floorboards, or if I'd get to him first.

Mr. Van walks me to the door. "I noticed you working in a notebook today, Lev. Your poem caught my eye."

"The 'I Am' poem?"

He shakes his head. Bryan thinks Mr. Van's black-and-white beard makes him look like a badger. His deep voice recites my words back to me.

" 'He pushes off, rolls like a log on a river, with me dancing, trying to stay afloat.' "

"Sometimes I write down lists and stuff to go with my drawings," I say. "It's nothing."

"I hope you'll come see me if you ever want to talk about those 'lists and stuff,' " Mr. Van says. "It is a gifted poet indeed who can draw such vivid pictures with words."

He writes me a hall pass and sends me to algebra. When I take out my math binder, I think about opening my wrestling notebook too. Maybe Mr. Van is on to something. But this is one of the few classes I don't have with Spence. I decide to pay attention.

When the last bell rings, I rush to pack up, slam my locker closed, and run outside. Instead of getting on the bus, I wait on the grass in front of school until I spot Bryan in the crowd.

I act like I'm going to give him a friendly slap on the back, but before he can blink, I've got his neck wrapped up in the crook of my arm. My leg hooks behind his brand-new Vans. Bam! He's on the ground, shoulders in the grass, our backpacks tossed aside.

"I give!" Bryan says.

I laugh and pull him to his feet before one of the bus monitors can yell at us for fighting. Meadowbrook Middle should have wrestling time built into the school day. I feel better already.

We pick up our backpacks and run for the bus. Miss Janice has sports radio blasting. She closes the bus door behind us. "You got grass in your hair, Lev. You two wrestling again?"

"Unfortunately," Bryan says. He brushes a leaf off his hoodie.

"Where were you last week?" I ask Bryan as I slide into our seat and crack a window. "You said you'd tell me on the way home. I've been waiting all day." Bryan was out for five whole days, and he never misses school.

He pushes his gelled bangs off his forehead. It's his new, middle-school style. I told him it looks ridiculous, but he says he's not taking fashion advice from a guy who wears a wrestling singlet.

"My uncle died," he says.

"Sorry." I look down at my backpack. Am I supposed to hug him now? We've been friends since second grade, but we're not big on hugging.

"We went to California," Bryan says. "That's where Uncle Steven lived."

"Wait a minute. Is this the uncle you used to watch pro wrestling with?"

Bryan nods. "He promised we'd go to WWE Raw next time he came to Baltimore. And before you say anything, Lev, I know it's not real wrestling. But that's what we liked about it. Uncle Steven said it was like watching the Three Stooges with a turbo shot of pain."

I groan. "Wrestling's not supposed to be fun. It's not supposed to be staged."

In real wrestling, there's no script. Your opponent can throw anything at you. That's why we practice three times a week. I can hear Coach Billy's voice in my head: *You win right here, in the practice room.* When we step out on the mat, he wants us to be ready.

"Yeah, yeah," Bryan says, rubbing his glasses on his hoodie. "I know. It cheapens the sport. You told me a million times."

Maybe if I tease him, he won't be so sad about his uncle. "If you love wrestling so much—"

"No way. I am not joining your team. The minute wrestling season starts, you have exactly zero life."

A grin takes over my face. We've had this argument so many times, it's turned into a joke between us. "That's the way I like it. School. Boom! Homework. Boom! Practice. Boom! Sleep like a rock and do it all again."

"What's wrong with goofing off?" Bryan asks.

Sometimes I wonder how we stay friends. Bryan's allowed to do what he wants with his free time, as long as he practices clarinet and keeps his grades up. Not me. My mom thinks the more scheduled my life is, the better.

I stand up and put my face by the window. "I smell the tang of winter."

Bryan snorts. "That's not the tang of winter. That's bus exhaust and your pizza breath."

"That smell is the taste of me wrestling at States." I sit and lean closer to Bryan. "This is my year. I'm going to train. I'm going to run every day before school." I shove Bryan's shoulder to wipe the smirk off his face. "Laugh all you want, doofus. I'm serious."

"Reality check: You're eleven years old. You've got more baby chub than muscles."

"I was this close last year." I hold my fingers a centimeter apart. "One move. I lost by one move."

"It was six months ago, is all I'm saying." Bryan isn't paying attention anymore. There's sheet music in his lap. He runs a finger along a line of notes.

"Nine," I say. I shake Bryan's arm. "I've had nine months to plan my revenge."

He makes an exasperated sigh. "Dial back the drama,

Lev. Forget about Spence. If States is your goal, it should be *your* goal."

I shake my head. "All the good kids on our team go. I have to be one of those kids or Spence will never shut up about it." I lower my voice. "I can't lose again."

"You're bugging out and the season hasn't even started yet."

"Hello? Have you met me?"

"Yeah. But I like you better when you're regular Lev, not Wrestler Guy."

"If I make it to States this year, will you come watch?" Bryan never comes to my matches. Not once since Mrs. Torres made us reading buddies in second grade and we got to be friends.

Bryan halfway frowns, so I know he's faking. "I don't know. There's no costumes."

"Nope."

"No masks. No flying suplexes. No battle cages."

"Anything else?"

"No cheerleaders."

"Ew. Are you really going to come to a match?"

"If you get to States, I'll be there."

I don't even have to close my eyes to see it. I'm on the mat at the state wrestling championship. The ref raises my hand in the air while Nick Spence cowers next to me, defeated. And there, in the stands, is Bryan, pumping a fist in the air.

CHAPTER 3

Mickey

It's our big night. We're officially moving up to the Eagles travel team. Kenna comes over after school to get ready for the meeting.

"Keep your eyes closed, or you'll ruin the surprise," I tell her, pulling her toward my closet.

Kenna jiggles her feet. Her dark curls jiggle too. She was quiet at school today, but there's nothing to worry about. Everyone on the team knows my family. Evan and Cody were Eagles in middle school. I've known Coach Spence practically my whole life. He's a serious coach. It won't be like rec league, with games of dodgeball and Steal the Bacon at the end of practices. Our teammates will be some of the best wrestlers in Maryland.

Hanging on the closet door are two Wonder Woman wrestling singlets, red with the yellow *W* logo. Singlets are one-piece uniforms, a spandex combination of a bathing suit and bicycle shorts.

I squeeze Kenna's hand. "Now," I say.

Her dark eyes flutter open. They widen in surprise until they're as round as gobstoppers. "Wow."

I do not hear exclamation points. I do not hear hearts, or grins, or any other kind of emojis in Kenna's flat "Wow."

"Awesome, right?" I ask, hoping she loves the singlets so much that she's gone into shock. "My mom found them," I hurry to explain. "She said they'll give us wrestling superpowers."

Kenna gapes at me. "We're not wearing these for real, Mickey. Tell me we're not."

"Don't you like them?"

She reaches out to stroke the smooth spandex. "Sure. For fun."

"Of course!" For a second, I thought Kenna hated the singlets. "They're not for competition, obviously. We'll have royal-blue singlets with the Eagles logo. But we could wear these to practice."

"I don't know." Kenna frowns. "It was super nice of your mom, but they're a little babyish." She rushes to get her thoughts out before I can argue with her. "We're in middle school. We'll probably be the only girls on the team again. We should try to fit in. They're kind of . . ."

Wonderful? Amazing? I think.

"Loud," says Kenna.

I cross my arms and scowl at the singlets, but really I want to scowl at Kenna. I was excited about wearing something special to our meeting. Even if no one else saw the yellow *W,* it would make me feel brave and strong instead of worried and awkward about joining a new team, not to mention worried and awkward about wearing a sports bra under my singlet for the first time. Kenna's mom took us shopping last week. I don't really need a sports bra, but Kenna sure does.

For a second, a thought flashes through my head. Maybe we should have stayed on rec with Coach Brandon. We were two of the best wrestlers on his team, the Mustangs. If one of the boys teased us about wearing sports bras, super-hero singlets, or anything else, they'd end up pinned to a wrestling mat by not one, but two girls.

But I blast the thought of Coach Brandon and the Mustangs out of my head. I am determined to be an Eagle like my brothers. Dad says if I make it through this season, he'll sign up to be an assistant coach next year. Then he'll have to spend more time with me.

Kenna nudges me, but I'm not about to smile. "We can be Wonder Women on the inside," she says. "That's where it counts, right?"

"I guess." I hand her a hairbrush. Kenna sits on the end of my bed and I settle onto the floor.

I wish Kenna were my sister. My brothers' idea of affection is a swift punch in the arm. Cody can barely sit still long enough to talk to me. And I hardly see Evan since he moved in with Dad over the summer.

"Why am I braiding your hair?" Kenna asks. "I thought we weren't wrestling tonight."

I nod. "It's just a meeting. Coach will go over sportsman-ship rules and introduce all the new kids. Don't be afraid of him. He only sounds like he's going to explode."

Kenna catches my eye in the long mirror next to my closet, raising her eyebrows at me.

I point to a picture of my favorite Olympic wrestler taped to the glass. "Four Dutch braids, please. Like hers."

She leans down to rest her chin on top of my head. "Are you sure we're ready?" she asks. "Wrestling in rec league was fun, but the travel kids are going to crush us."

"No way," I say. "We've got this."

"I don't know. Remember what Coach Brandon said? Starting travel is like moving up to middle school. We're going to be the new kids again. We're going to lose. You hate losing."

"Maybe we'll lose at first. But it won't last forever. We're strong. I only gave up three matches last season."

She rolls her eyes at me, so I elbow her knee.

"Still," Kenna says, "are you moving up to travel because you love wrestling, or because your brothers love wrestling?"

Wrestling is my family's thing. When my parents divorced, Dad put all his attention on wrestling. He's the one who takes my brothers to their weekend tournaments and signs them up for summer camps with famous wrestlers. Mom said the only way I'd get to spend time with him was if I went along to watch my brothers compete. Ever since then, I've wanted to be a wrestler like Evan and Cody, like my dad was in high school. It's in my DNA.

I study Kenna's hair in the mirror. Kenna is biracial. She looks like both her parents. Her hair isn't straight like her mom's or thick and wiry like her dad's. It's a jumble of tight brown curls, a shade darker than her skin.

17

I don't look anything like my dad, with his red hair and sharp jaw. He says I'm Mom's Mini-Me. My hair's plain brown and straight. I have her brown eyes. The only thing that stands out about me is Mom's cleft chin. And her dimples, but only when my smile is really big, and smiling like that shows off my braces. No thanks.

I wish I had Dad's red hair, like Evan, instead of looking so average.

I sigh and smile at Kenna. "I've dreamed of being an Eagle my whole life."

She wraps an elastic around the last braid. "Kids at school are going to think we're weird."

"They'll think we're awesome!"

I pop a bicep. Kenna closes her eyes and shakes her head.

"You promised," I remind her. "When we signed up for Eagles, you said you were all in."

I jump up to get a closer look in the mirror at the four fat braids running from my forehead to my neck and down my back. "Perfect!"

"Dickinson isn't like elementary school," Kenna says.

"It's middle school. What did you expect?"

"I don't know what I expected." She falls back on my bed. "It's hard work."

There's something I'm not getting. Lately, when it comes to Kenna, it's like I know the first steps of a math equation but can't figure out how to finish the problem. She's met a bunch of new kids. She keeps inviting them to sit with us at lunch, as if we're interviewing girls to be our friends. Is that what she means by hard work? Because it feels like it to me. Things are easier when it's the two of us.

I pull on her arm. "Promise me you won't quit."

Delgados aren't quitters, but Kenna's not a Delgado. Sometimes she needs convincing. "We don't care what anyone says about girl wrestlers, remember? We have each other. We're Wonder Women. Even if we don't wear the singlets."

"I guess. As long as we stick together," Kenna says.

"Best friends and wrestling partners forever." Makenna and Mikayla at school. Kenna and Mickey on the mat.

CHAPTER 4

Lev

I'm so pumped for the Gladiators preseason team meeting tonight. I jump off the school bus and run home, leaving Bryan in the dust.

"Wait up!" he calls.

I turn and jog backward. "Can't! Got to get ready." I put up my hands T. rex style and growl at Bryan. He runs to catch up to me.

Bryan's not a bad athlete. He used to play soccer. But when the league made kids try out and placed them on A, B, and "We Don't Care" teams, Bryan was done. He says sports should be for fun, not for glory.

"Do you think we'll get to write horror stories for Mr. Van's new project?" Bryan asks. "I'm going to write about a haunted restaurant where all the food comes to life."

"Can't you stop thinking about food for a second?" I turn around to walk with Bryan, fixing my backpack so my books sit high on my shoulders. Coach Billy says if we have to carry heavy backpacks, we might as well build up our neck muscles.

"The guy has more books on his desk than our whole media center," Bryan says. "Okay. I exaggerate, but if Mr. Van weren't a giant badger man, he'd get crushed by a book avalanche. I can picture it. He's staying late at school, grading essays. There's no one else in the building. Suddenly, a breeze wafts across his stack of books."

"Wafts?"

"Don't interrupt the flow of my literary genius," Bryan says. "The books teeter. Mr. Vanderhoff is wrapped up reading the brilliant writing of one Bryan Hong. He does not notice disaster is about to strike. Then, ka-BOOM!" Bryan pauses.

"It hits him like a tsunami?"

"Exactly. Mr. Van is knocked unconscious. They don't find him until morning."

We stop at the bottom of my driveway. "I thought you liked Mr. Van."

"No one is safe from the word stylings of Bryan Hong."

"Oooh, I'm scared." I pretend to shake. "See ya!"

"Yeah," Bryan says. "See you in a few months."

"It's not that bad, Bry. We eat lunch together every day."

Bryan shrugs.

"No practice on Tuesdays or Thursdays. We'll ride bikes."

"It's a deal. Unless it snows. Then, video games at my house."

"Mom!" I call the second I'm in the door. "Is my Gladiators hoodie clean? I want to wear it to the meeting."

Grover waddles into the hall, snuffling my backpack. He sounds more like a pig than a dog. I pat his soft ears.

"You're old enough to do your own laundry," Mom calls from the top of the stairs.

Mom thinks being a middle schooler means I should be more independent. When I started sixth grade, she started her master's degree. She says she wants to be a school guidance counselor when she grows up. I hope she sticks to little kids. My mom is way too nice for middle school.

Mom comes down the stairs. She's dressed for class, corduroys and turtleneck sweater. Her hair is pulled into a bun. She's even wearing makeup. Mom says she wants the professors to know she's a serious student. In one motion, she ruffles my hair, picks up my backpack from the floor, and hangs it up on its hook.

"What's in here? Rocks?"

I stand in front of Mom to make sure she can't run off to do laundry or hunt for the psych textbook she's always losing. "Will you help me with my homework plan?" I ask. "I want to get it all done before we leave."

Mom's starting to pull folders out of my backpack when I hear a chair move in the kitchen.

"Dalia's home?"

This is the only time of day when I have Mom to myself, before everyone gets busy with sports. I know I've lost her attention as soon as my sister strides into the hall. Dalia is supposed to be at field hockey. She's a junior in high school, which means every second of her day is scheduled with homework, SAT prep, and sports. Mom treats Dalia like she's a VIP guest in our house. Abba says Mom's acting this way because my sister's going to college soon. I can hardly wait to be an only child.

Dalia wears her hair in a long, tight braid. It swings back and forth like the pendulum in that horror story Mr. Van read to us.

"Forgot my cleats," she says.

Mom starts tearing through her purse, looking for car keys.

"I don't need a ride, Mom," Dalia says. "Evan's driving me."

"Evan's coming over?" I run to the window. Evan is Dalia's boyfriend, and he's the best. He loves video games and plays touch football with me in the yard, and he's a wrestler. He even won state champ in eighth grade.

"Forget it, Lev," Dalia says. "Evan's taking me to practice. That's it." She shoves hockey sticks into her tall, narrow bag. A horn beeps. Dalia runs outside in her socks, cleats swinging from her hands, braid swinging on her head.

"Wait!" I follow her outside.

Evan rolls down the window of his silver truck. "Hey, buddy." He gives me a fist bump. Evan has curly red hair and a cleft in his stubbly chin. He has a wrestler's wide shoulders and neck, and the tops of his ears are lumpy in places. I'll never have beat-up wrestlers' ears. Mom and Abba make me wear headgear, even at practice.

"You training yet?" Evan asks.

I'm about to tell him the team meeting is tonight, but Dalia interrupts. "No wrestling talk," she says. "Sometimes I think you only go out with me so you can hang out with my baby brother."

I'm not a baby, I'm about to complain, but Evan points a thumb at my sister and shrugs at me. I know what he means: *Sorry, buddy. She's the boss.* His eyes crinkle like he's holding in a laugh. Evan is the exact opposite of Dalia, funny and easy to get along with. Everyone in my family likes him.

As I watch the truck pull away, I smile. I'm going to work my butt off this season. By the time I finish middle school, I'll be a state champ just like Evan.

CHAPTER 5

Mickey

When we get to the high school where the Eagles practice, I skip through the halls.

Dad says wrestling is a growing sport in Maryland. Our county runs a league of rec-level teams and one travel team, the Gladiators. Teams practice at high school gyms, but there are a few independent teams, and Dr. Spence's Eagles is the best one, with the toughest training program. That's why Dad picked the Eagles when Evan and Cody were in middle school.

Mom grins at me and Kenna as we head to the gym for the meeting. "It's a big step, moving up to travel," she says. "You girls are going to be fierce."

She's still wearing her conservative work clothes—slacks and a plain maroon sweater. Mom is the principal's secretary at St. Matt's Catholic Prep, where Cody is a freshman. Evan would have been a junior at St. Matt's if he hadn't moved in with Dad and switched to public school. St. Matt's is coed, so I'll go there for high school too. One of the perks of Mom's job is discounted tuition.

"Oh, the sacrifices I make for my children," she likes to say, faking a dramatic sigh.

Kenna walks behind us, hugging her arms to her chest. Her mom is supposed to join us here so we can all go in to the meeting together.

"Mikayla, stop skipping," Kenna says in a loud whisper. She looks up and down the hall, where some boys in basketball jerseys straggle by their lockers. "Can you at least try to act cool?"

"We're at wrestling. You have to call me *Mickey*," I say. I spread my arms wide. "I'm finally an Eagle." I swoop like a bird toward the gym door. And crash right into Coach Spence.

"Oops," I say. "Hi, Coach."

When Dr. Spence was Evan and Cody's coach, I thought he looked like a dog. It's the way his face strains forward from his thick neck.

I peek around him into the gym. Chairs are set up for the Eagles families, but hardly anyone is here yet. We must be early.

I haven't been listening to Mom and Coach's conversation, but now I pay attention. Coach sounds like a barking dog. Words burst out of him a few at a time.

"I loved coaching your boys, Suzanne," he says. "Good kids. Lot of talent. But this is a competitive team."

"The girls *are* competitive," Mom says. Her lips have disappeared into a thin line. What did I miss? Mom says in a pleading voice, "John, you've known Mikayla since she was five. And Kenna's been her training partner for years."

"It's not about Mikayla or Kenna," Coach says. He looks at his clipboard. "I hear they're both good technical wrestlers, for girls. But girls don't have the physicality to roll with my guys. It's not a safe environment for them."

Kenna shrinks next to me. Her shoulders slump.

Mom starts to argue, but Coach cuts her off. "If Mikayla wrestles competitively now, what about high school? She can't join the St. Matt's team. You think they'll let her wrestle boys at a Catholic school?"

"That's beside the point," Mom says.

I hear Kenna's mom coming down the hallway, her high heels tapping. She stops and takes in our faces. "What's going on?"

I like Mrs. Franklin. She teaches science writing at University of Maryland, and she's super fashionable. Tonight, she's wearing a long red wrap that sweeps across her shoulders. She'll get Coach Spence to change his mind, I'm sure of it.

Mom says, "Apparently, girls are not welcome on the Eagles wrestling team."

Mrs. Franklin gives Coach Spence her don't-mess-with-the-professor face. "You made us come all the way down here with the girls for this? We signed them up weeks ago."

"I sent an email," Coach says.

"Where did you send it?" Mom asks.

Mrs. Franklin shakes her head. "This is unacceptable. Don't you know how disappointed they'll be?"

Coach Spence's face turns bright red. The color spreads to his balding forehead, making his blond crew cut look almost white.

Kenna buries her face in her mom's wrap. I ball my hands into fists so I won't cry.

As the adults argue, a boy comes down the hallway. He's way too young for high school. Dirty-blond hair flops over his eyes, boy-band style. He's wearing an Eagles jacket, the blue one with white leather sleeves that Cody begged for but we couldn't afford. The boy gawks at us until Coach barks, "Inside, Nick." Then he slides through the gym doors.

Nick. I know who that is—Coach's son. Cody warned me that he's a stud, a big wrestling talent with the attitude to match.

"You sent it to the DelgadoFamily email? John, Paul and I have been divorced for years. You know I don't use that address."

Coach Spence shrugs. "Honest mistake."

I look at Mom. *Do something!* I shout at her, but only in my mind.

"I'm going to speak with the head of the wrestling league," Mom says. "You may be willing to give up on our girls, but I am not."

"Suit yourself, but I'm on the league's board."

Coach gives Mom a quick nod and disappears into the gym. Families are starting to come in for the meeting. People who know Evan or Cody wave to my mom as they pass.

"Let's get out of here," Mom says.

Mrs. Franklin bundles Kenna against her body and walks ahead of us to the parking lot. My mom doesn't hold me. She's too angry. I can tell because she's stomping.

Once we're outside in the late October cold, we all stop moving.

Mrs. Franklin speaks first. "Don't waste your breath speaking with the league, Suzanne. I don't want Kenna wrestling for that man."

Mom puts a hand on Mrs. Franklin's elbow. "I feel responsible," she says. "We've always trusted John. He was a good coach for the boys. I'll find another team. One that's more welcoming."

I tug Mom's sleeve. "What other team? The Gladiators are the only other travel team in the county. They're our rivals. We can't join the Gladiators. Right, Kenna?"

But she won't look at me.

"I'll call you tonight," Mrs. Franklin tells Mom.

In the car, Mom is so quiet that I know she's still arguing with Coach Spence in her head. I press my face to the cold window and stare at the passing lights.

When we get home, Mom's phone rings. She goes into her room and closes the door. I hope it's Coach Spence, calling to say there was a mistake. He does want me and Kenna to be Eagles, after all.

Finally, Mom calls me into her room. After Dad left, she redecorated. She said she wanted her room to look like a summer garden. The walls are a warm shade of peach. The bedspread has a pattern of flowers.

When I sit next to Mom on the bed, she pulls me close. "Mikayla, honey. Kenna wasn't sure about wrestling this year. Did you know that?"

I shake my head. My eyes crinkle. That can't be right. Kenna is as excited about moving up to travel as I am, except for the Wonder Woman singlets.

"Mrs. Franklin is worried that other coaches are going to be like Dr. Spence. That they'll give you girls a hard time."

"But we have each other. Anytime a boy doesn't want to practice with us, we have each other."

"She thinks wrestling travel will be too stressful for Kenna. Starting middle school is a big enough transition."

Tears start to slide down my cheeks. "She's my partner. She can't quit."

"You can go back to rec," Mom says. "It's not too late. You know how highly Coach Brandon thinks of you."

I have to make a decision.

I have always followed behind my brothers. Much as we tease and beat on each other, it's all play. I've always done what my parents told me. Mom's got enough worries, and I'm afraid if I tell my dad no or speak my mind, he'll get mad and won't see me. At school, I do every piece of homework, study for tests, and follow the rules. And at wrestling, if Coach says to do twenty push-ups, I do all twenty.

But being a rule follower and a hard worker, that's not enough for Coach Spence. I have to ask myself, am I going to give in, go back to my rec team, as if being the best wrestler isn't important to me? I can either give up now, before the season starts, or push ahead, with or without Kenna.

I pull away from Mom and stand up. "I'm wrestling travel. Even if I can't be an Eagle."

Mom runs her hand down my braids. "We'll find you a

good coach. But I'm not going to lie. Wrestling is a small world. Coach Spence will be at tournaments. You'll compete against Eagles wrestlers. It's going to be a tough season."

"I am tough, Mom."

She rubs her temples. "What are your brothers going to say?"

"Coach Spence has bigger problems than my brothers." I pop a bicep.

Mom laughs and kisses the tip of my nose.

A plan is already forming in my head. While Mom finds me another team, I'm going to work on Kenna. Dealing with the Coach Spences out there will be a whole lot easier with my best friend by my side.

CHAPTER 6

Lev

When Abba and I get to the school gym, I look for Josh Kim and Isaiah Oliver, my best friends on the Gladiators. Coach Billy calls us the Fearsome Threesome. Isaiah and I nicknamed him Billy the Kid because he's one of the youngest coaches in our league. Coach Billy is Josh's uncle, and Josh makes a huge deal about being respectful. He hates it when we call Coach Billy the Kid, even when he shows up to tournaments in jeans and flannel shirts. Mom says Coach missed his calling. He dresses like a country music singer.

But tonight Coach is ready to wrestle. He's got on red shorts with the Gladiators helmet logo, and an old gray T-shirt. He's busy pushing a mop around, disinfecting the mats. He stops and leans against the top of the handle when he sees me, putting out a hand for a shake.

I haven't seen Coach since the end of last season. Am I still mad at him for telling me to take a shot against Spence, for making me lose that match? My stomach clenches like a fist. Yep. Still mad.

"We're expecting a great season out of this guy," he tells

my father. Coach reaches down to mess up my hair. "Getting a little shaggy there, Sofer."

I shudder, but Abba laughs. He's been after me to cut my hair for weeks.

Josh and Isaiah aren't here yet, so I head up to the top of the bleachers to put my wrestling shoes on. But when I open my bag, the first thing I touch is my notebook.

I've had a wrestling notebook since rec league. I used to get really nervous at meets. Once, I chewed the collar of my T-shirt until the stitches came loose. Mom asked my rec coach to come to our house and talk it over. I remember how small Abba's coffee mug looked in Coach Harvey's big, dark hands.

"A distraction between matches is good for the little guys," Coach Harvey said. "Keeps their minds busy." He noticed my drawing of Grover on the fridge. "Hey, you're a good artist, Lev. Why not try a sketch pad?"

The next night, Abba gave me an extra Hanukkah gift, my first wrestling notebook. I started writing down the things I saw, drawing cartoons of people at tournaments, and making lists of moves I wanted to learn. Coach Harvey was right; the notebook does keep my mind off being nervous. Seeing the words and pictures on paper means the thoughts aren't in my head.

I close my notebook and lean against the cement wall. Up here, I can watch everyone coming in. I see Isaiah's mom, Mrs. Oliver. She's tall, like Isaiah, and dressed in her *Gladiators Mom* shirt. Mrs. Oliver tracks who's going to which tournaments and who's in what weight class, and keeps the whole team organized. If she's here, Isaiah is around somewhere.

Finally, I spot him. Isaiah and Josh are swinging Isaiah's little brother, Devin, by his wrists and ankles, like a hammock. Devin laughs as they drop him to the mat, then pile on top of him.

I'm so happy to see them, it pushes the old, angry thoughts about Coach Billy out of my mind. Yeah, I'm going to work hard and kick Spence's butt this season, but with Josh and Isaiah here, I know I'm also going to have fun. They're a big part of why I keep coming back, practice after practice, even in February when it feels like the season will never end.

I'm about to run down there and join them, when a girl with two long braids pulls herself to the top of the bleachers.

"Nice view," she says. She's wearing an *Eagles Wrestling* sweatshirt. I ignore her and pull the ankle straps on my shoes tight.

"I'm new," she says.

Wait. She's new. As in, new to our team? I give her sweatshirt the eye. "Could've fooled me."

She looks down at the Eagles logo on her chest. "It's my brother's."

"Okay," I say. But my voice makes it clear, it's not okay.

"What weight class are you?" she asks.

"Don't know yet."

"Yeah, right. Wrestlers always know."

I size her up. She looks about my weight. Maybe a little taller and skinnier.

"I'm Mickey. Who are you?"

"Lev." She sure asks a lot of questions. But I've got one for her. "Why aren't you wrestling with your brother?" Wrestlers are loyal. If you're lucky enough to be from a wrestling family, every kid wrestles for the same team.

"I've got two brothers. I thought I'd be an Eagle like them, but the coach won't let me join." She puts her elbows on her knees and leans forward. "No girls allowed."

I've wrestled girls a couple times, but that was back in the rec league. There aren't many girls wrestling travel. And we've never had a girl Gladiator before. Still, I say, "That stinks," because it does. If I had a brother, I'd want to be on the same team as him. "Are your brothers moving to Gladiators too?"

She shakes her head. "They're in high school. Cody wrestles for St. Matt's Prep. Evan, he's the oldest, he used to go to St. Matt's, but now he's wrestling for Clifton High."

That's Dalia's school. I look at the girl. Her face is familiar, even though her hair is brown, not red. "I know a guy who wrestles at Clifton. Evan Delgado. He's my sister's boyfriend."

"That's my brother! You know him?"

I nod. "You're lucky. Evan's the best. I wish I had a brother."

"Some brother. I didn't even know he had a girlfriend." She leans against the wall and crosses her arms.

"Well," I say, hopping off the bleachers. "Welcome to the team." Why didn't Evan tell me his sister was joining Gladiators? I decide to set her straight. "Coach Billy's not going to take it easy on you just because it's your first practice." *Just because you're a girl* is what I don't say.

She hops down too. "Bring it on."

I find Isaiah and Devin sitting in a pile of wrestling bags. Devin lunges at me, but I grab his arms and lean down to grapple with him. He's a six-year-old version of Isaiah, same long, skinny legs. Devin slips away from my hold, but he falls on his butt. Isaiah and I laugh so hard, I don't notice a hand grabbing the back of my neck.

"Josh!" I shout. I spin to face my wrestling partner. He gives me a noogie before letting me loose.

"You ready?" Josh says. Last season, we were all in the same weight class. That's when Coach started calling us the Fearsome Threesome. Josh is about my height, but he's heavier. I bet he'll wrestle 100 or 110 this year. Someday he'll be built like Coach—thick chest, wide shoulders, strong legs.

"Ready," I say.

Josh shoves Isaiah. "You'd better stop growing," he jokes. "There's a height limit for the Fearsome Threesome."

"My dad wants me to partner with one of the older kids this year," Isaiah says. "I'm supposed to challenge myself."

"What? We're not challenging enough?" Josh says.

Isaiah catches him in a headlock. "Next question?"

One of Abba's favorite sayings is *You're only as good as your partner.* He said the same thing as Isaiah's dad, that I should ditch Josh and find a more experienced wrestler to train with. Maybe later in the season. Right now, I'm happy to be back with my friends.

The three of us join our teammates jogging around the wrestling mats.

Josh jabs my shoulder. "Is that a girl?"

I look around the room for Mickey. There are kids near her, but they move around as they pass, never getting too close. "Stick your eyes back in your head," I say. "You know that Delgado kid, the one who was on the Eagles?"

"Yeah?"

"She's his sister."

"Bet she's good," Isaiah says.

Coach blows his whistle. "Skip!"

Fifty wrestlers, from tiny six-year-olds to eighth graders with facial hair, skip around the mat. The youngest Gladiators are mostly brothers of boys on the team. They've been around the sport and skipped rec league.

"Roll to a shot!"

I duck into a somersault. As soon as I'm right side up, I lunge forward and stretch both arms in front of me, as if I'm grabbing an invisible opponent. Mickey's across the room. She's watching me, doing what I do. I don't care, as long as she stays with the other new kids.

By the time Coach calls, "Bring it in!" I'm wiping sweat off my forehead. The team stands in a circle around him.

Coach's eyes move from boy to boy. "Wrestling is the sport of philosophers and kings," he says. "A Roman emperor once said, 'The wrestler must ever be ready on his guard, and stand firm against the sudden unforeseen events of his adversary.'"

I straighten up. I'm ready. On my guard against my adversary. *Look out, Nick Spence. I'm coming for you.*

Coach describes what he expects in the preseason, which is drilling, drilling, and more drilling. "That's how you build the muscle memory you need to perform on the mat," Coach says. Then he looks right at Evan's sister. "Mickey, front and center."

I can tell she doesn't want to be singled out. She looks at the mat, braids hanging over her shoulders. On the bleachers, she seemed tough, but she looks small next to Coach.

"I got news for you guys," Coach says. "This kid has more courage in her little finger than the rest of this team put together. I'm going to say this one time and one time only. Mickey is a Gladiator. If I catch you mouthing off to her, going easy on her, if I catch you treating Mickey like anything other than your teammate, you're running laps. Understood?"

Nods and mumbles. Mickey squirms like she wants to crawl under the bleachers and hide.

"Understood?!"

"Yes, Coach!" we all shout.

I feel bad for her. When I moved up from rec to travel, my old teammates stayed behind with Coach Harvey. It took a while to make friends.

Coach motions for everyone to come close. We stack our hands in the middle. I notice that Josh and some of the other kids don't touch Mickey's fingers.

"On three," Coach Billy says. "One, two, three—"

"Gladiators!"

"Pair up, pair up. Sit-ups first," Coach calls.

Josh and I wave good-bye to Isaiah, who taps the shoulder of an eighth grader. We find an open spot on the mat. I try to focus, but Mickey's walking around the room looking for a partner. Everyone ignores her. Jerks. Coach finally calls her over. I'm relieved, until she heads in my direction.

"Coach says you're wrestling with Milo," Mickey tells Josh.

I hear a couple of nearby eighth graders sniggering. My cheeks burn, and it's not from all the running we've done tonight.

Josh looks at me, shaking his head, but he doesn't say anything. We both know Coach's rule: No complaining on the mat.

Mickey lies on her back. I'm supposed to hold her ankles for sit-ups, but I freeze. "Wait. I'm training with you?"

"You got a problem with that?"

Yeah, I do. Evan's sister seems nice, but this is wrestling. Nice doesn't cut it. I don't need the guys laughing at me. I'm supposed to wrestle someone faster, tougher, stronger than I am. How am I supposed to train for States if my partner is a newbie—and a girl?

We make it through conditioning, but I'm still stuck with her when Coach calls for live wrestling.

I kneel on the mat. Mickey puts her arm across my waist and wraps her fingers around my elbow. I can't pull away when she leans her chest against my back.

Wrestling girls in elementary school wasn't a big deal. Nobody cared or said it was weird. But things are different between boys and girls in middle school. It's awkward, even with girls I've known forever, like Emma Peake. Having a strange girl leaning on my back, her arm wrapped around my middle, is not exactly comfortable.

I wait for Coach's whistle, determined to show her I'm not here to mess around. I don't want to be the first guy in the room to get beat by a girl.

CHAPTER 7

Mickey

The first thing I notice about the Gladiators is speed. Even when they're messing around before practice, these boys are spinning, sprawling, diving to take a shot on their partners, scooping up legs and ankles so fast I don't see it happen until they're on the ground, fighting for control.

No one tells us it's time to start. Even the little kids know, you lace up your shoes, put your headgear on, and start jogging around the mats. I watch my new teammates and copy what they're doing, trying to act like I'm not totally confused. The last words Mom said when she dropped me off were "Have fun." Ha. The way these guys are pretending not to stare at me, I can tell it's going to be a while before wrestling with the Gladiators is fun.

Heavy-metal music blares from speakers I can't see. It's ridiculous, the way boys weave around me as they jog, like I've got cooties. If Kenna were here, we'd be laughing at the way they're tripping over themselves to avoid me. But I have no one to laugh with. For the first time in my life,

I don't have a friend in the wrestling room. That kid Lev doesn't count, even if he does know Evan.

My new coach, Billy Kim, calls us to the center of the mat. He's Asian American and the youngest coach I've ever had. There is no question Coach Billy is a wrestler. Those banged-up cauliflower ears mark him. Damaged cartilage in the ears is permanent.

"Mickey, front and center," Coach says.

Uh-oh. This is not how it's supposed to go.

Ignore me, I think. *Treat me like I'm any other new kid on the team.* But I might as well have *GIRL* tattooed on my forehead.

Coach's "treat Mickey like everyone else" speech has the opposite effect. When it's time to pair up for conditioning exercises, every kid I get close to suddenly finds another partner.

Dad always says wrestling is a sport that "takes all comers." If you're willing to step on the mat and compete, it doesn't matter what color you are, how much money your parents make, or if you have a disability. So why are these kids acting like they've never seen a girl before?

Coach Billy grabs my shoulder. He points at Lev and his partner. "See that kid over there? The one who looks like me?"

I didn't notice before, but Lev's friend is a mini version of Coach Billy. He's too old to be Coach's son, but they must be related.

"Tell Josh to partner with Milo," Coach tells me. "You're with Lev."

To say Lev and Josh are not thrilled about splitting up

is an understatement. Josh shakes his head as he stalks away.

Coach calls, "Sit-ups!"

I lie on my back. Lev's supposed to hold my ankles, but he stands there, his big dark eyes staring down at me.

"I'm training with you?"

"You got a problem with that?"

Lev kneels, grabs my hand-me-down wrestling shoes— he's careful not to touch actual female skin—and slides the rest of his body as far away from me as possible.

I want to shout, *You think I wouldn't rather be wrestling with my friend?* But it's no use. He doesn't care that Kenna quit on me and left me to deal with these jocks by myself.

When I see Kenna at school, I would love to tell her off. Instead, I'll have to pretend everything's fine. Because if I get mad and say she's a big, fat quitter, I'll never convince her to join the Gladiators.

The last half hour of practice is live wrestling, when all the partners compete as if we're in real matches. Lev takes down-man position, kneeling with his butt on his heels, his arms propping his chest up. I look down at him before I take the top spot. He's got too-long wavy brown hair and freckles on his neck. He looks more like a little kid than a teenager. I bet he's in sixth grade, like me. His Gladiators T-shirt has the team logo on the back, a gray helmet with a black feathered plume. It says *Give It All You've Got.*

I kneel and place my right arm around Lev's stomach, left hand on his elbow, ready to move on Coach's whistle. When I lean against Lev's back, he jerks away. What's he afraid of? It's not like I have much chest to brag about. What I do have is smooshed down by my new sports bra. If we're going to be partners, he'd better get over it.

Coach Billy yells, "Bottom man, you've got thirty seconds to score!"

On the whistle, I yank Lev's elbow to the side and press down on his back, trying to flatten him to the mat. I can't let him escape and earn a point, but he's strong. I sprawl my legs out to get traction, push from the toes of my shoes, and hold tight to his middle. Thirty seconds feels like forever.

"Switch positions!" Coach yells. "Top man on the bottom."

We continue like that until practice is over and my T-shirt is soaked with sweat. I'm sitting by myself, unlacing Cody's old wrestling shoes, when I hear Lev's voice.

"She didn't score on me, but she's fast," he tells Josh and his other friend, a tall black kid.

If Kenna were here, we might smile at each other and high-five. Instead, I walk by myself out of the hot gym, into the cold November air.

"How was it?" Mom asks before I even have a chance to buckle my seat belt.

"Fine," I lie.

She turns to look at me. "Are you going to be okay without Kenna?"

It's only the first night of preseason, and this was the most intense wrestling practice of my life. I'm starving and lonely and angry all at the same time. Am I going to be okay without Kenna? Probably not. But I have to keep it together so I can tell her how awesome it is to be a Gladiator.

I take a deep breath. My body's so warm, the windows steam up. "There's still time for Kenna to change her mind," I tell Mom. "Coach Billy's fine. The guys on the team are really good."

Mom frowns. "And if she doesn't change her mind?"

I shrug, even though Mom's eyes are on the road.

"I'm not sure how I feel about you being the only girl on the team," Mom says. In the rearview mirror, I see worry lines marching across her forehead.

"It's fine, Mom. I'm used to it, remember? Evan? Cody?"

No matter how tough it gets, I can't quit wrestling. Ever since Evan moved in with Dad, this sport is the glue that keeps our family together.

The next day at school, I rush to lunch. I know exactly what I'm going to say to Kenna, how I'm going to describe the Gladiators to make her realize how much she misses wrestling.

But Kenna has her own news. "I'm joining drama club," she says. Her arm is linked with Lalita Parsons.

Lalita went to a different elementary school. She's been taking ballet and tap classes since she was little. But now she's into hip-hop. She's trying to talk her parents into letting her take lessons.

Even though she wears sweatpants with the word *DANCE* across the butt, it's hard not to like Lalita. She's enthusiastic about everything, whether it's her favorite K-pop boy band, the book we're reading in language arts, or Dickinson Middle's sloppy Joe sandwiches.

Lalita leans across the table. "I'm getting an act together for the talent show. We're doing the 'Thriller' dance. It's super fun. And it's easy to learn. You should do it too, Mikayla." When she smiles, her braces are electric blue. They match her glasses.

I shake my head. "No time. Not till wrestling season's over." I'm surprised that I'm actually sad about this. It's been a long time since Kenna and I took dance together. Learning the Thriller would be awesome.

Lalita looks confused. "Wrestling season?"

"Yes!" Kenna answers. Her smile is so big that I forgive her a little. "Mickey, I mean *Mikayla* is a great wrestler." She leans closer to Lalita. "You should see her on the mat. She crushes kids. Even boys."

Lalita's eyes widen behind her glasses.

Kenna's compliment should make me happy, but I'm still upset about last night's practice. With the Gladiators, I'm starting over from the bottom. There are second graders on that team who are better than me.

"Lalita asked me to do makeup for the dance," Kenna is saying.

" 'Thriller' makeup? You mean zombies?"

She nods and her curls bounce happily. "I've been watching YouTube videos. I can already do blood and bruises." She takes out her phone and clicks through the photo gallery. There are pictures of Kenna with dark circles under her eyes and a dripping, bloody nose. Kenna with flakes of decaying skin peeling off her face.

"I didn't know you were into makeup," I say. "How'd you make that flaking skin look so real?"

Kenna smiles. "I need someone to practice on besides myself." She flutters her eyelashes at me. It's a BFF thing. She knows I can't resist.

"Sure," I say. "I'll be your zombie guinea pig." Everyone at our lunch table thinks that's hilarious.

Since there's no wrestling practice on Tuesdays, Kenna comes over after school. We carry her new stage makeup kit to the upstairs bathroom.

"What kind of zombie do you want to be?" she asks.

I shrug. "Maybe I died of boredom."

"Just for that, I'm going to give you a head wound." Kenna gets out a jar of soft, clear wax. "It's what they use in movies, for special effects."

How does she know that?

Kenna smiles. She looks happy, leaning against the bathroom sink with a palette of eye shadows in one hand and her brushes in the other.

"What?" I ask, as she dabs purple shadow on my eyebrow.

"It's nice hanging out with you and not talking about, you know."

"Boys?"

"Wrestling. For a long time, all we talked about was wrestling. We used to do other stuff together, remember? Ballet and tap class. And that time when we wanted to start a cupcake company."

I do remember. Kenna and I were still dancing when

47

we started to wrestle. It was fun, except when Mrs. Franklin yelled at us for wearing tap shoes on her hardwood floors. I liked tap, especially the kicks and stomps. But performing in front of people made me want to vomit. And then there was that time I came down to breakfast wearing a tutu over my wrestling singlet. Cody still teases me about it. Kenna and I decided not to sign up again. Or maybe I was the one who decided to quit, and Kenna didn't want to keep dancing without me.

"We still bake," I say. "Every time you sleep over, my mom lets us take over the kitchen."

"I guess. But a business would have been fun. I still have that list of cupcake flavors we came up with in fourth grade."

"Mmm. Black licorice. We could still do that."

"When?" Kenna asks. "You're at practice three times a week. You'll be wrestling every weekend until spring."

It's harder for us to spend time together since middle school started. If I can't get Kenna to join the Gladiators, how are we going to stay friends?

"Look." Kenna turns my body toward the mirror and I see a different person. A scarier person.

"Too bad Halloween is over," I say, admiring my sunken-in eyes and bloody forehead.

"I call your look Prom Scream. Get it? Like prom queen?" Kenna admires her work. "Please do the talent show with us, Mickey. I'll find you a dress. An ugly pink one with lots of lace."

"I wish I could. I miss you at wrestling," I tell her. When

she starts to argue, I say, "It's not about being partners. I like having a friend on the team."

This summer, we went to wrestling camp together for the first time. There was a boy in our group whose arms only went down to his elbows. He was a good kid and a strong wrestler. I wonder if the boys who wrestle me feel the way I did, that there are unspoken rules when you're on the mat with someone whose body is different from yours, but nobody's supposed to say anything. I was glad Kenna and I could talk about it at the end of the day, when her mom drove us home.

Kenna studies my face. Now she has this secret life with a vocabulary I know nothing about. Until middle school started, we were always together. How different could we be after just a few weeks?

A lot, I tell myself.

CHAPTER 8

Lev

Ever since Gladiators practice started, I'm hungry all the time. When the lunch bell rings, I pound down the stairwell in a herd of sixth graders. We have four hundred kids in our grade, Meadowbrook Middle's biggest class ever. I rush around the corner, pushing through the crowd. On Tuesdays, the cafeteria serves square pizza. It's a slice of heaven.

Bryan's in his usual spot at our table, but he's not eating. His eyes are glued to the cafeteria door.

"It's pizza day, Bry. What are you doing? Get in line before all the corner pieces are gone."

Bryan springs up and walks as fast as he can to the pizza line. I lean back and watch where Bryan's going. Who do I see walking to the pizza line ahead of him? Marisa Zamora. I should have known.

"Hey, Sofer." Nick Spence and his friend Darren Warshauer are standing at the end of our table. Nick tosses his hair. He must think some girls are watching.

I take a bite of my pizza and chew it at them.

"Heard you got a new teammate." Nick's keeping a

straight face, barely, but Darren's smile shows all his braces. He's in the jock group, which wasn't even a thing in elementary school. Typical Nick, acting like a jerk to impress the cool kids.

"I've got a lot of new teammates," I say. It's not a lie. There are at least eight new Gladiators, but I know who he's talking about.

"Only one of them is a girl," Darren says. "I don't know whether to be grossed out or jealous." His light-brown hair is gelled like Bryan's, but it looks cooler on Darren.

Nick's face twists into a smirk. "It's not natural. Wrestling is a man's sport. That's what my dad says, and he's on the board of the county wrestling league."

"Shut up," I tell them both. I've barely spoken to Mickey since that first practice, even though Coach keeps pairing us up. I keep telling myself if I don't talk to her, she'll give up and find someone else to train with.

Bryan slides into his seat and drops his tray on the table. Pizza. Tater tots. Applesauce.

"Is it true Sofer's got a girlfriend?" Nick says. "If you can call her a girl." He elbows Darren.

"Who? His partner?" Bryan looks at me. "I thought you hated her?"

I take a deep breath. *Uh-oh.*

"She's your partner?" Nick breaks into hysterical laughter. "That is perfect. Sofer and the She-Man are wrestling partners." He and Darren walk away, shoving each other. They look back at me and start laughing again.

"What'd you do that for?" I ask Bryan.

"What's the big deal?" he says through a mouthful of pizza. "She's not your girlfriend."

"And she's not going to be my partner either, not for long." I chew my pizza. "There's got to be something I can do."

"Besides not speaking to her?" Bryan asks. "You really have a way with the ladies."

"Like you do?"

Bryan blushes from his chin to his glasses. "I talked to Marisa."

"So?"

He wants me to do the guy thing, clap him on the back or shake his hand.

"I'm paving the way," he explains. "I'm going to ask her to the winter social."

"If you're such an expert on girls, how do I get rid of Mickey?"

Bryan folds his arms across his chest. I know he's annoyed, but I want to talk about his crush about as much as he wants to talk about my wrestling problems.

"The silent treatment's not working," he says. "Why don't you cut her a break? She's Evan's sister. Evan's like your big hero wrestler brother. If you're nice to his sister, he'll make you his official sidekick."

"Ha ha." I don't want to think about what Evan will say when he finds out I'm not speaking to Mickey.

"Maybe she's nice. She must have a sense of humor to put up with you."

I shake my head and we both go back to eating. Two rows over, Nick and Darren turn to look at me. The whole jock table bursts into laughter. Bryan's too busy gawking at Marisa to notice.

No matter what Nick thinks, my problem's not only that I'm stuck wrestling a girl. Mickey's new to travel. Partnering with a newbie stinks. How am I going to get better unless she's pushing me to work hard and improve?

All my anger at Coach Billy, all the hard words I should have said to Spence push their way into my throat. "You don't understand," I tell Bryan. "It's a sports thing." I'm being a jerk, but I can't stop myself. "I'll ask my wrestling friends. Your advice is useless."

Bryan blinks at me from behind his glasses. "Then don't ask me next time." He stands, grabs his trash, and walks out of the cafeteria.

All my good feelings about this season, my plans for making it to States, disappeared when Mickey Delgado walked into our wrestling room. It's her fault Nick Spence is laughing at me. It's her fault I argued with Bryan. I wish she'd just give up and quit already. But so far, no matter what I throw at her in practice, Mickey keeps coming back.

CHAPTER 9

Mickey

Once a month, if no one has a wrestling tournament, my family goes to church together, and then we make a big Sunday dinner. Kenna thinks this is bizarre, because divorced parents are supposed to hate each other. But my mom and dad are friends. After all, they've known each other since they were in high school. Besides, before she died, my grandmother made them promise they'd continue our Sunday tradition.

"Why change a good thing? We're still a family," Nonna used to say. She also used to say my parents are proof that opposites attract. Where Mom is soft and plushy, Dad is prickly and hard, from his scruffy beard to his lean muscles. Ever since the divorce, Dad's been obsessed with sports. He's not the only one. A couple of years ago, *Sports Illustrated* called our part of Maryland "Sportstown USA." It feels like every kid in my school plays soccer, lacrosse, or football. In summer, they all swim. Wrestling hasn't caught on like that yet.

My dad has done CrossFit, has trained for mud runs,

and is addicted to watching *American Ninja Warrior*. At first, Mom thought he was doing it to "impress girls." Yuck. But neither of them has dated anyone for more than a few months. It's hard not to wish they'd get back together.

Now that they're just friends, Mom and Dad get along. Except when Dad pulls one of his stunts, like getting matching tattoos with Evan when he turned sixteen. When Mom saw *Delgado* inked in huge letters across Evan's shoulders, she went ballistic. Cody can't wait for his sixteenth birthday, when he'll be old enough to get his shoulders tattooed. He only needs one parent to sign the forms. Mom is furious, but we don't talk about tattoos, or anything else my parents disagree about, not at Sunday dinner.

Dad leans against the stove as I stir the cheese mixture for Mom's stuffed shells. "I've been reading the wrestling forums online," he says. "A lot of people think you should be allowed to wrestle for any team in the league."

Mom snorts. "Tell that to the Spences."

"John Spence thinks it's his job to maintain certain traditions," Dad says.

"But what do *you* think, Dad?" I ask.

He crosses his arms, looking at Mom, not me. "Girls can wrestle in rec league, sure. But there's a lot of talent on the travel level. The competition is tough."

"I'm tough," I say. I can't believe Dad agrees with Coach Spence.

Cody and Evan squeeze into the kitchen, hoping to swipe meatballs from the sauce pot.

"The Spences have a point," Evan says.

"Thanks a lot." I pretend to flick ricotta cheese at him.

Evan crunches a carrot stick at me. It's as orange as his hair. "I'm on your side, sis. But what are you going to do when you get to high school? St. Matt's is coed, but they are not ready for girls to compete with guys. Especially not in wrestling."

Cody's mouth is filled with a stolen meatball. Mom whacks him on the arm with a wooden spoon. "You'll ruin your appetite."

He swallows, grinning. "Coach Spence is a dinosaur," he says. "Wrestling is changing and he doesn't want to see it. When I was an Eagle, I wrestled girls at tournaments. Not a lot, but there were some."

Soon everyone is talking over each other. Don't they get it? There is only one female wrestler in this house. Me.

We sit down for dinner. Dad puts a stuffed shell and two turkey meatballs on my plate, then covers everything with homemade sauce. It smells amazing. But when I open my mouth to take a bite, words pour out.

"Why is it okay to keep me off the Eagles just because I'm a girl?" My brothers stare at me, but I keep going. "When kids of different races wrestle each other, nobody cares. And wrestlers with disabilities, like that boy at my camp. Everyone cheers for them. Why am I 'that weird girl who wants to wrestle against boys'?"

Mom puts her napkin down. Dad pushes food around his plate. Cody's the only one nodding in agreement.

"There was a girl in my weight class last year," he says. "She was so fast, I never had time to think, 'Uh-oh. I'm wrestling a girl. Better be careful not to touch . . . certain areas.' "

Oh, no. I know Cody's trying to help, but his story just took a wrong turn. He blushes bright red. Evan struggles to keep a straight face.

Mom only makes it worse when she says, "There's nothing wrong with the word *breasts*. The meatballs on your plate are ground turkey breast."

Cody nearly chokes.

"I was trying to talk about something serious," I say. I look to my father for help. "Dad, please."

"What? I thought this was the evening's entertainment," he says.

He puts an elbow on the table, arm up. Cody shrugs at me, puts his elbow down too, and grabs Dad's hand. Evan cheers on their arm-wrestling match.

"You're a pack of animals," Mom says.

I try to catch Cody's attention, tell him to cut it out, but he's too busy trying to wrench Dad's arm out of its socket. I push my plate away.

It's the Delgado Brother Effect. Laugh first, think never.

I want to talk to my family about the Gladiators, whether I should stick with a team that doesn't want me around and put all my effort into wrestling when I don't have Kenna to share it with. But I can't risk talking to my parents. If I heard right in the kitchen, Dad's still not sure I have the skill to wrestle travel with boys. If my family doesn't take me seriously, how am I going to make it through this season?

It's my turn to wash up, but Evan grabs a dish towel and

leans against the counter. When I hand him the giant salad bowl, he pretends to drop it.

Evan can be a pain. Half the time, he jokes around, doing stupid stuff to make me laugh. As I wash plates, I wonder if something's going to upset him. I never know when Evan's mood will turn dark, when he's going to start picking a fight with Mom and stomp out of the house without saying good-bye.

Evan hated going to the school where Mom works. He said it was bad enough having Mom monitor his homework and screen time at home, but when she started showing up in his study halls and lunch periods at St. Matt's, that was when the arguments got bad.

On the day he moved out, Evan told Mom, "I can't breathe around you." He told me, "A man needs to live with his father." Whatever that means.

My shoulders slump, as if I've been washing dishes for hours. "None of the boys on the Gladiators talk to me," I tell Evan. "It's too hard without Kenna."

"Did you tell Mom and Dad?"

I look at my brother. He has Dad's red hair, but we share Mom's square face and cleft chin. Somehow, the features that look so plain on me make Evan handsome. It's not fair.

"Didn't you see what happened at dinner?" I ask him. "The second I tried to talk about it, everyone started laughing and arguing. Besides, if I complain about wrestling, Dad will tell me to suck it up. And Mom? She'll be on the phone with Coach, telling him to make the team apologize to me."

Evan puts his hands up in surrender. We're quiet for a minute, working side by side at the sink.

"Have you ever wrestled a girl?" I ask.

"Couple of times."

"Was it weird?"

Evan pushes his hair out of his eyes without thinking about it. How come he's so good at being himself, when I'm totally awkward?

He says, "The first time was at a high school tournament. When I saw a girl's name on my bracket, I figured I had an easy win."

I nod. I've heard boys say that about me and Kenna plenty of times. "She kicked your butt, didn't she?"

"Pinned me in the second period. I took it easy on her. That was my mistake, and she made me pay for it. You ever do that when a guy underestimates you?"

"No mercy." I put my hand out for a fist bump. If kids look at me in that I'm-better-than-you way, just because they're boys, it's over before they know what hit them. Usually a cement mixer—my favorite move—is what hit them.

Evan shoves me. "Way to be, Mighty Mite."

When Evan's easy to be around like this, I can forget how bad things were between him and Mom last spring. Our house is calmer since he moved in with Dad, and it gives Evan what my history teacher calls *perspective*. He understands things that Mom, Dad, and Cody don't see. Evan knows I'm upset about the Eagles. He knows I need to talk.

"You're a Delgado," he says. "Start winning matches and the guys on the team will warm up to you."

When he says "guys on the team," Lev's face flashes in my mind. That's right! Evan doesn't know about Lev. I whap him with the dish towel. "Guess who my partner is?"

"Stone Cold Steve Austin?" he jokes.

"I'm talking about real wrestling." I smile big enough to show my braces, because I've got the goods on Evan.

"Hit me."

"Lev Sofer. Your girlfriend's brother." I draw out the word *girlfriend* with extra attitude.

Evan's eyebrows just about leap off his face. "Don't tell Mom, Mickey," he says. "If she finds out, she'll pester me until I bring Dalia over to meet her. She'll ask me stuff, like what we're wearing to prom." He scrubs his forehead. "Mom and I are just starting to get along better. You can't tell her."

"Fine." I feel bad for Evan, and he's right about Mom, but I still get to tease him. What are little sisters for? "What'll you give me? Chores for a month? Money?"

"Better than that. I'll talk to Lev. He's my buddy."

I cross my arms over my chest.

"Trust me," he says.

"I do."

That night, Mom comes to my room and sits on the edge of my bed. "Dad and I were talking about you."

I don't answer.

Mom picks up Spike, the plushy hedgehog I've had since I was a baby. She strokes Spike's fake fur. I hear all the things she's not telling me, that Dad's not convinced I can make it

60

on a travel team. That Mom is all for girl power but doesn't want me to get hurt.

"It would be easier if you still had Kenna," Mom says. "I felt safer when it was the two of you."

Tell me about it. I prop up on my elbow. "What does Dad say?"

More than anything, I want Dad to be on my side. I want him to get it, that I'm all in for wrestling, just like Evan and Cody.

Mom sighs. "He says Delgados aren't quitters. And that he's proud of you."

"Then I'm sticking with it."

CHAPTER 10

Lev

We only have a few more practices before the Eagles' big Thanksgiving tournament. It's the first wrestling event of the season, my first chance to show Nick Spence I'm ready to win. I push myself at practice. When Coach tells us to jog, I run. When he says, "Twenty squat-jacks!" I do an extra five.

Mickey tries to keep up with me. She's not bad for a noob, no matter what Josh says. He's still mad at Coach for splitting us up. Josh grumbles about his new partner, a pudgy fifth grader named Milo.

"Milo's strong, but he's so slow, it's like wrestling a bag of mashed potatoes," Josh says. He glances at Mickey, who's sitting by herself near the parents, snapping headgear over her braids. "At least *she's* halfway decent."

Isaiah nods. "She'd wipe the floor with him."

I lean down to tie my shoes so Josh and Isaiah won't see me blushing. Not because I like Mickey or anything gross like that. I'm embarrassed because, even though we're partners and Mickey's good for a first-year Gladiator, I still haven't spoken to her much since the first practice. How would I even start being nice to her now?

"Coach should stick all the new kids together," Isaiah says.

Josh sighs and stands up. "Uncle wants us to teach the noobs 'The Gladiator Way' or some garbage. If we show them how things are done around here, maybe we'll get our old partners back."

"The sooner the better," Isaiah says. "I'm sick of you two complaining."

We jog around the mats to warm up. Coach Billy blasts music to keep our energy pumping.

By the time I get home from practice, it's nine o'clock. I'm glad Mom made me do my homework right after school. Even though it's quiet in the kitchen while I eat my bowl of cereal, my head echoes with the music and noise of the practice room.

"Headache," I tell Abba. My headaches are worse this season. The kitchen light is too bright. I close my eyes.

My father is my favorite person on the planet, but if I had to choose a second, it's my Gran's wife, my other Gran. I call her O.G. for short. She's chill and fun and rides go-karts with me at the beach every summer.

O.G. is so calm and fun to be around, it's hard to believe she helped raise my mom. Mom is always rushing from one emergency to the next. Sometimes the emergency is real, like when her best friend had breast cancer and Mom organized meals for her kids. And sometimes it's just that no one in the house has clean underwear. But Mom acts as if everything needs her full attention Right Now. It's worse since she went back to school.

Abba's not like that. He is calm. He's got black hair with silver streaks and rosy cheeks like a little kid. Abba's father is from Israel. They lived there for a while, when Abba was my age.

Abba's parents, my Saaba and Safta, retired to Israel. We see Gran and O.G. pretty often, but I've only ever been to visit Israel twice. I don't remember much. Palm trees, desert, blue doors in Jerusalem. Every few years, Saaba and Safta come to Maryland and stay for a few weeks. It's easier for them to come here, because of our sports.

I wonder if having a parent from another country is what makes Abba different. When I ask him a question, it's like time slows down. Abba stops what he's doing and settles in to listen.

Now he's looking at me in the bright kitchen light. "Of course you have a headache, Lev, sitting in all that sweat." He kisses my wet hair, which I still haven't cut short for competition. "I'll take care of the dishes. Go shower." He pushes me up the stairs. "When you're done, Dalia wants to talk to you."

"She does?" My sister never wants to talk to me.

Abba shrugs. "Your guess is as good as mine."

I find Dalia sitting on her bed, phone in one hand, homework spread around her. Grover is snoring on the floor. Dalia's bare toes dangle above his furry back.

"Abba said you want to talk to me."

I haven't been in her room in a long time. Dalia has a

64

new *University of Maryland Field Hockey* poster on her wall. She's determined to go to UMD after high school. Her closet door is open. I see clear plastic boxes marked *COLLEGE*. I guess Dalia is as excited about leaving home as I am that she's going.

Mom and Abba keep telling her that no matter how good she is at field hockey, sports scholarships are hard to get. She knows her best shot at money for college is good grades. So she's always working. Whether it's sports or school, Dalia has to be the best. One thing I like about wrestling? It's something my sister would never do. Something she'll never be able to beat me at.

"I hear you're wrestling with Evan's sister. Mikayla, right?" Dalia asks.

Is that her real name? It makes Mickey sound like one of the lip-gloss-wearing, giggling girls in my homeroom.

I nod.

"He says she's a good wrestler."

"She's okay."

"Is she better than you?"

"No." Bryan would call my laugh a *scoff*.

I lean down to pet Grover's ears. He rolls over for a belly rub, so I sit on the floor next to him.

Dalia raises one thin eyebrow at me. "Evan wants you to be nice to her."

"What do you mean?" As if I didn't know.

"It's not easy for her. Her best friend quit. Evan said they've been training partners for years. Mikayla's never been the only girl on her team before."

I shrug. "Her problem."

Dalia nudges my shoulder with a bare foot. Her face is all bones and angles, especially when her dark hair is pulled back with athletic tape. She undoes her braid, combing it out with her fingers. "Evan says he'd hate to see her quit wrestling."

"She wants to quit?" That's what I wanted, isn't it? But my eyes feel hot. I try closing them. The headache pounds. "What am I supposed to do about it?"

"You're the softie in the family, Lev, not me," Dalia says. "You could start by talking to her."

"Maybe," I say.

Yesterday at school, Nick stuck a paper heart on my locker with the initials *LS + MD*. If I'm nice to Mickey, what if Josh and Isaiah stick hearts in my wrestling bag or make kissing noises behind my back at practice? Forget that.

When I get into bed and take out my notebook, I can't concentrate on what I learned at practice tonight. I'm thinking about Dalia, how things used to be before she turned into Miss Annoyed Teen USA.

The two of us used to play Uno 500 every summer. We brought our cards everywhere and kept track of points in the loser's hand. The first person to get five hundred points was Loser of the Year. We played on the long car ride to the beach house we rent with Gran and O.G. We played after lunch on rainy days. It took the whole summer. The last time we did Uno 500, Dalia was Loser of the Year. She didn't even get mad. She laughed and said she'd get me next time.

Then Dalia started summer field hockey, going to Disney

World tournaments with her club team instead of coming to the beach house. That's when our family changed. One of our parents was always driving or flying somewhere with my sister. And because she had practice, or her team was going to a tournament out of state, we hardly ever had Shabbat dinner on Friday nights anymore.

Abba, Dalia, and I used to bake challah on Thursdays after school so the bread would be ready to eat on Friday. Every Thursday, I'd rush home to get my homework done. Dalia put all the ingredients out so when Abba got home from work, we could start baking. Sometimes he let me proof the yeast. That was my favorite part. I loved watching the dried flakes of yeast plump up and fizz in warm water, knowing that they were going to turn our flour into delicious bread. This past summer, Abba and I only made challah a few times. Dalia wasn't there to help.

Our family is changing. We're busy with wrestling, and field hockey, and the papers Mom has to write for graduate school. I miss Friday nights when we sat and ate and talked about the week. I think I'm the only one who's noticed we've lost the habit of making special bread for Shabbat, saying our Friday night prayers over candles.

Mickey's mother shows up at the next practice. I watch her from the bleachers. Ms. Delgado is kind of chubby, but otherwise she and Mickey have the same square face, minus the braces and wrestling headgear. My mom hardly ever stays at practice. She says she's not the wrestling mom type. Which is dumb because I'm a wrestler and she's my mom. But Mom says she'll never get used to this sport. It's too violent for her. She doesn't come to practice, doesn't make friends with the other parents. Abba brings me to meets and tournaments. He doesn't mind hanging out with team dads.

We have a preseason scrimmage against the Eagles tomorrow. Coach wants us to wear our Gladiators singlets. He takes every meeting with the Eagles seriously. Billy the Kid used to be assistant coach for the Eagles. He left so he could head up the Gladiators. Josh says his uncle and Nick Spence's dad argued. I guess Dr. Spence wanted Coach Billy to be his assistant forever. Now our two teams are rivals. There's nobody Coach Billy wants us to beat as bad as the Eagles.

We all strip down to our boxer shorts and pull on the singlets that Ms. Delgado and Mrs. Oliver are handing out. Our singlets are red, with the gray and black Gladiator logo on the chest. Down our backs, there's one word, written in gray: *GLADIATORS*.

Josh and Isaiah are whispering. I roll my eyes at them. Nobody cares that we're walking around in our underwear. Wrestlers weigh themselves at every competition, sometimes at practice too. There's no privacy, but we're used to it. Or we were, when our team was all guys. Over by the parents, Mickey's mom is handing her two singlets. She points to the gym door. I forgot. Mickey can't try on her singlet in here with the rest of us.

I don't like the way Josh and Isaiah are watching her.

Dalia said Evan wants me to be nice to Mickey, so I shake

my head at the guys. Why can't they leave her alone, act like she's not here? Mickey's not making a big deal about seeing us all in our underwear. But Josh and Isaiah are.

"Let's follow her," Josh says. "I want to see where she's going."

"She's going to the girls' room to change, you idiot," I say.

Josh ignores me and stands up. Isaiah follows him out of the gym.

Stay out of it, I tell myself as I step into a singlet and pull it over my chest. I check to make sure the shoulder straps aren't too loose, that the elastic on the thighs isn't too tight. But then I remember what Bryan said at lunch, that day we argued. *Why don't you cut her a break?*

I leave the gym in my singlet and jog down the hallway. Isaiah's leaning against the girls' room door. Mickey tries to reach past him for the door handle, but he shifts his long body to block her. Josh grabs the singlets out of her hands. He holds them behind his back, where she can't reach.

Mickey sticks her chin out. Her hands are in front, ready to make a grab.

"I'm not afraid of you," she tells them.

"Leave her alone," I say.

Isaiah scoots away from the door, says, "C'mon, Josh," and goes back to the gym.

Josh glares at me from under his dark bangs. "I thought you wanted to be my partner." He hands over the singlets. Mickey slips into the girls' room.

"I don't have much choice," I whisper, in case she's

listening. "She's a decent wrestler. We should give her a chance."

"Whatever," Josh says. "Come on. If we hurry, we can wrestle each other while she's changing."

I shake my head. "I'll wait for Mickey."

He gapes at me like I'm a traitor or something, then runs to catch up with Isaiah.

Did I do the right thing? Mickey's tough. Maybe she won't like me any better for sticking up for her.

When she comes out in her shorts and T-shirt, she holds the singlets behind her back, as if I might grab them. "Are you okay?" I ask.

"I'm used to it." Her eyes are bright and glassy, the way Dalia's are when she's had a fight with Evan.

"I'm sorry."

I wanted Mickey to get annoyed and ask for a different partner. But that was because I didn't want to wrestle a noob. I didn't want to deal with the guys teasing me for wrestling a girl. How did ignoring her turn into this?

I can't look her in the eyes. "I should've been a better partner."

"Obviously."

I follow Mickey to the gym. "My sister said you're thinking about quitting."

"What do you care?"

"You're good," I tell her. "For a first-year Gladiator, you're really good."

It's true. I beat Mickey most of the time when we're live

70

wrestling, but that's because I'm stronger. She's quick, and she picks up new moves faster than I do.

"I have to be better than good if I want your friends to leave me alone." Mickey stops outside the gym door. "So you're on my side now?" she asks. "For real, or because my brother asked you?"

Better than good. That's what I have to be if I'm going to beat Nick Spence and make it to States. That's when I realize, she may be a noob and a girl, but Mickey is the best partner for me. Every time she walks into practice, she has to prove herself. She understands better than anyone what it means to work hard and push yourself.

"For real," I say. I put out my hand. "Shake on it."

Mickey's grip is tight. "Partners."

CHAPTER 11

Mickey

I want to put the so-called Fearsome Threesome nonsense behind me. My mom always says boys will be boys. But that's a stupid excuse for acting like idiots.

Even though it's late when I get home from practice, I ask Kenna to video chat.

"It's an emergency," I say in my message. We talk while she sketches makeup ideas for the "Thriller" zombies.

"I'm tired of boys," I tell her. "I can't get away from them. They're in my house. They're on my team. Ugh."

"Try sharing a bathroom with a five-year-old. He pretends he's swimming in the bathtub. And he has bad aim," Kenna jokes.

I laugh. Her little brother Caden is more adorable than annoying.

"Multiply that by fifty," I say. "I'm one girl in a room full of fifty foul-smelling, sweaty boys."

"But how's the wrestling?"

I still feel like I have to prove myself every time I walk into the practice room. I'm still showing them that a girl can work as hard as they do. But I don't tell Kenna that. I haven't given up on her. Maybe if I make the Gladiators sound awesome, she'll come back. "You'd love it. Coach teaches us new moves every week. Cool stuff we never did in rec. Ankle picks and duck unders."

"Whoa."

I don't tell her that I'm afraid to make a mistake. The last thing I need is for Lev, his friends, or anyone else to catch me messing up. I don't tell her we ran sprints relays for so long the other night, a kid threw up.

"I wish you were coming to rehearse with us," Kenna says. She holds up a drawing, a bony face with green hanging-off skin and matted hair.

"That looks . . . horrible. Perfect and horrible."

Kenna wishes me luck and we sign off. My first competition without her is tomorrow. I miss her like missing the summer when it's cold outside and you think spring will never come.

The next morning, I feel better about the scrimmage, ready to show Dr. Spence I'm travel team material.

Kenna and Lalita have a surprise for me, a digital file for my phone. They created a playlist of songs to help me get pumped for the tournament. The last track is Michael Jackson's "Thriller." While I'm on the mat today, Kenna will be dancing and laughing with Lalita and our middle school friends, but I can't get upset about it. I'll save "Thriller" for later.

During the drive to the community center where we

have county dual meets, my friends send me texts that say *Grrrl Power!* and *No Mercy*.

Mom's driving. Evan and Cody have a preseason tournament in Pennsylvania and, of course, Dad wanted to go with them.

When we arrive, I check in with Coach Billy, and Mom finds Mrs. Oliver, Isaiah's mother. It's not fair that she has a friend on Gladiators and I don't. My mom collects friends the way normal people collect teapots or action figures.

"How're you feeling, Mickey?" Coach Billy asks. I can see why Lev and his friends call him Billy the Kid. He's wearing jeans, a flannel shirt over a Gladiators tee, and a knit cap. Maybe he thinks that goatee makes him seem more mature, but Coach doesn't look much older than Evan.

"I'm awesome!" I say. But suddenly, I'm sick-to-my-stomach nervous.

"I know you've got some history with the Eagles." Coach Billy glances at Mom. She sends him a little wave and a big smile. Then Coach puts both his hands on my shoulders and looks right in my face. "It's better to get it over with. You'll be seeing more of these guys at tournaments once the season starts."

"Yes, Coach."

Maybe I'll feel better if I try talking to Lev before the meet starts. He's not exactly a friend, but on the Gladiators, he's all I've got. It doesn't take long for me to spot him sitting on top of the bleachers.

"Nice view," I say.

"You said that last time."

"Still true." Even though it's not. I'm looking at a sea of blue. Eagles wrestlers cover the mat, warming up and stretching. "How's the scrimmage going to work?" I ask.

"Same as a regular dual meet," Lev says.

Dual meets are my favorite part of wrestling. Unlike tournaments, where you compete as an individual athlete, dual meets are two teams' best wrestlers battling it out. You earn team points for minor decisions in close wins, major decisions when you win by eight points or more, and technical falls when one wrestler is up by so many points that they stop the match. You get the most points for your team if you pin your opponent, so everyone is out for the pin.

When Kenna and I were on the Mustangs, dual meets were so much fun. Because it's only one match at a time, Coach Brandon lined us up at the side of the mat to watch. We clapped and yelled for our teammates. At tournaments, there are so many matches happening at the same time, it's hard to feel like a real team.

Lev opens that notebook he's always carrying and draws a chart for me. "These are the weight classes. One kid from the Gladiators wrestles one Eagle at each of the weights. It's not like a tournament. Only weight matters, not age. A ten-year-old who weighs 105 could be up against an eighth grader. Although Coach doesn't usually do that." He scratches his forehead with his pencil.

"Hold up," I say. "You wrestle 95, same as me. How come we're both wrestling today?"

Lev nods. His too-long hair falls in his face, shaggy and brown. "Coach asked me to wrestle up today, so you could get a match in." He frowns. "I was hoping I'd get to wrestle Nick Spence."

"You know him?"

"We go to the same school. He hates me."

"Why?"

"I don't know. I should be the one hating him. We wrestle each other every year and he always wins. He's obnoxious about it too."

"I know kids like that." When you're a girl in a boys' sport, you get to see bad sportsmanship front and center.

Lev sighs. "He knocked me out of a state qualifier last season. I've got to beat him this year. Nothing else is going to make him shut up."

"But why are you wrestling up today? My dad says you never want to wrestle someone who has five pounds on you."

"We needed someone at a hundred. I know we're not supposed to keep score at a scrimmage, but Billy the Kid wants to beat the Eagles. Bad. Josh told me he's not going to forfeit any points."

"So who are you wrestling?"

"Josh tried to get a look at Coach's clipboard, but he guards that thing like an armored car."

I smile. My top lip curls up over my braces. I hate when that happens.

"Hey," Lev says. He leans in, staring at my face. "Your braces are red and gray."

"Gladiators colors. I had the bands changed last week."

Every time I look in the mirror and see red and gray on my teeth, it reminds me that I'm a Gladiator now.

"That's cool. Hey, Josh! Isaiah!" His friends are sitting at the bottom of the bleachers, playing a game on their phones. I follow Lev as he bounces down the steps. "Check out Mickey's braces," he says.

I smile for them, which is awkward. Lev's acting like we're all friends now and it's not weird that these kids who weren't speaking to me three days ago are standing around staring at my mouth. I have never been so happy to hear Coach Billy blow his whistle. "Let's go, Gladiators!" I jog over to join the team.

Coach tells us a few wrestlers are coming late, so we're not going in weight class order. Lev has one of the first matches.

"Good luck," I tell him as he leaves to warm up.

Our team sits in folding chairs set on one side of the mat. The Eagles have matching chairs on the other side.

With Lev warming up, I don't have anyone to sit with. I try hanging out in the stands with Mom. I wonder if it's as weird for her as it is for me, competing against Evan and Cody's old team. It doesn't look like it. Mom may be angry that Dr. Spence kicked me and Kenna off the Eagles, but the way she's laughing with her old friends, I guess she doesn't blame them. I should ask her about it. Did any of Mom's friends on the Eagles stand up for me, tell Dr. Spence that he was wrong, and girls should be allowed to wrestle? If they did, no one told me.

Mom nudges me out of the bleachers. "Go join your team, Mikayla."

I take an empty seat at the end of the row, next to the youngest Gladiators. Little guys like Isaiah's brother Devin don't care that I'm a girl. They only see another big kid on their team.

I'm sitting close enough to Coach Billy's corner that I hear his advice to Lev.

"Think about your opponent," he says. "Your job is to outperform him, not only on the mat, but up here." Coach taps Lev's forehead. "Killer instinct."

Lev looks older with his shaggy hair pushed up under his headgear. His smile is gone. His eyes are intense and focused. I'm surprised that I'm excited. That's my partner stepping onto the mat.

It reminds me of wrestling rec with Kenna. I'd cheer for the other kids on the Mustangs, but when Kenna was on the mat, my heart beat harder. If she was losing, I almost couldn't watch. If she was winning, I'd scream myself hoarse.

Lev and the guy from the Eagles shake hands. I still can't look at the royal-blue singlet, with its gray eagle logo, without thinking, *That was supposed to be me.*

The ref blows the whistle.

Lev lunges as he grabs his opponent's leg, but the other boy steps back before he can get a hold.

"Lower your level," Coach calls.

Lev goes for it again. This time, he owns his opponent's leg, hugging it tight against his chest.

Across the mat, Dr. Spence watches from his corner. He's dressed up compared to Coach Billy: khakis, a blue Eagles fleece. Dr. Spence is quiet. Coach Billy is way more into the match. He leans toward the mat, miming the moves he wants Lev to make.

When the Eagles kid loses his balance and puts his hands out to break his fall, Lev is on him. I can't believe how good he is. I'm screaming, "Go, Lev!"

Isaiah taps me on the shoulder. "Coach says you're up soon. Come on."

I warm up, jogging along our side of the mat. My opponent should be warming up too. I try to spot him. I know it's a him, because, duh, no girls on the Eagles, but the only person near the mat is Nick Spence. As the last seconds of Lev's match tick down, Nick runs onto the mat holding a rolled-up, duct-taped towel. Sometimes refs get so into what they're doing, they don't hear the buzzer. When Nick touches the ref's shoulder with the towel, he blows his whistle. The match is over. The ref raises Lev's hand in the air.

Finally, it's my turn. Parents in the stands shout my name. Mom's voice pops out of the crowd. "Girl power, Mickey!"

I would be embarrassed, but I'm grinning around my mouth guard. Mom remembered to call me Mickey.

I jog to the center of the mat and try to ignore what's going on in the Eagles' corner. The ref is talking to Nick and Coach Spence.

I look at Mom. If she's noticed something weird is happening, she doesn't show it. "You got this!" she shouts.

I try to shake the worry out of my head, but now both

coaches and the ref are at the judges' table. They point to the Eagles' corner, where Nick is standing. Coach Billy's face is turning bright pink. After weeks of practice, I know what that means. He's about to start yelling.

Lev waves to me from his seat on the side of the mat. He gives me a thumbs-up. A buzz is building in the stands. Parents are talking, wondering why the match hasn't started. When the ref calls me to the center of the mat, I'm confused. I think I'm supposed to wrestle Spence, but he's still in the Eagles' corner.

The ref takes my hand and holds it high. "Eagles forfeit," he says.

Coach Spence nods without looking up from his clipboard. Nick tears off his headgear. He looks like he's about to throw it. If this were a real dual meet, a tantrum like that could get him kicked out. But Nick thinks better of it and jogs off to sit with his team. A little girl in a pink T-shirt comes up behind his chair and wraps her skinny arms around him.

I turn to Coach Billy. "I'm not wrestling today?"

Coach doesn't answer. He writes something on his clipboard.

"But why? Is he hurt?" I ask.

The next pair of wrestlers is already on the mat, taking their stances. I tug Coach's sleeve.

"I'm sorry, Mickey. They don't have to give a reason," Coach says. "Tell Milo he's on deck."

There's booing from parents in the bleachers. Mostly

Gladiators parents, but some Eagles too. They're not boo-ing me, are they?

I walk off the mat and slump in the chair next to Lev.

"What happened?" he says.

Isaiah leans over Lev to ask me, "Why did Spence forfeit?"

My brain is putting the pieces together. "Same reason they wouldn't let me join the Eagles, I bet. He doesn't want to wrestle a girl."

"That's not fair," Lev says. "You train as hard as anyone."

I take a deep breath. "It's happened before. Boys did it a couple of times when I wrestled rec." I can see that Josh, on the other side of Isaiah, is listening too.

"I'll wrestle you," Lev says. "We're both 95 pounds."

I frown. "Forget it. It's okay."

"Are you sure?"

I nod.

Mom is in the bleachers, trying to catch my eye. Her eyebrows shoot up in double question marks. She moves forward, as if she wants to fly out of the stands and res-cue me. I stare right at her and shake my head slowly until she sits down. I'll explain what happened later. Right now, I want to run to the girls' room and hide. Why did I think this would be a good idea? Why did I think, just because I'm on a different team, the Eagles would let me wrestle?

But I can't leave. Lev grabs my elbow and says, "We'll get back at them. We've got the whole season."

For the rest of the meet, Lev cheers on Gladiators wres-tlers with our team, but my voice stays stuck in my throat.

CHAPTER 12

Lev

I'm glad Abba came to the scrimmage with me. Mom would have asked a million questions. Since she went back to school, everything I do and say is her chance to practice being Nina Sofer, Future Guidance Counselor.

"That must be very upsetting for you, Lev," she says whenever I complain. About anything. There are times, like tonight, when I miss plain old Mom, who hugs me too tight and says what she thinks, instead of bouncing my feelings back at me like a ball I'm supposed to catch.

Mom doesn't understand my thing with Nick Spence. She doesn't like me and Dalia to use the word *hate*. But at school and tournaments, when I see Spence, my whole body tells me *Run! Get out now!* like he's a tornado about to smash me into pieces.

Abba thinks I'm making our rivalry into a bigger deal than it needs to be. He says Nick is a regular kid, a middle schooler just like me and not some invincible super enemy out of a comic book. But that's not how I see it. No one should get away with what he did to Mickey today.

"What happened with Mickey's match?" Abba asks as we drive home. "No one in the stands knew what was going on."

Even though today was just a scrimmage, the Eagles wanted to win as bad as we did. Coach Billy refused to tell any of the Gladiators how we did overall, since we weren't supposed to keep score. But I noticed he was smiling and laughing with the parents when Abba and I helped put mats away.

If Coach Spence is anything like Nick, he hates to lose. He'd never forfeit a match, even if it doesn't count. That's six team points in the trash.

"Spence forfeited on purpose," I say.

"Really?" Abba doesn't believe me. "What are the facts? No rumors."

"The Spences think wrestling should be all boys. Nick told me at school."

Abba shoots me a look in the rearview mirror.

"Also, Nick's not a nice kid. I told you. I keep telling you that."

"It's wrestling, Lev. No one wins a trophy for being nice."

It's frustrating when Abba gets like this. I want to be angry, to shout and maybe punch something, but he keeps being reasonable. "You know what I mean, Abba. He tells everyone at school that Mickey is my girlfriend. It's gross. And at tournaments, when the bout sheets are posted, he stands there waiting for me. And then he says stuff like, 'I'm going to crush you today.'" I don't remind Abba about fifth grade, how Nick told everyone he made me cry.

"He's all talk."

Not if he always wins, I think. I swing my legs and kick the back of the passenger seat.

Abba says, "Take Coach Billy's advice. Don't let Nick get in your head. If you train hard enough, any kid is beatable."

"How's Mickey supposed to beat him if he won't step onto the mat with her?" I argue. "She deserves to wrestle."

"All I've been hearing since practice started is how you're never going to make it to States with a girl for your partner. Something's changed."

I look out the window. The sun is going down, making the sky red and gold. Abba expects me to stand up to bullies, be a friend to that one kid in the cafeteria no one wants to sit with. He doesn't know, and I don't want to tell him, that's not how I've been treating Mickey. "I'm sick of guys picking on her, that's all."

"Maybe the forfeit had nothing to do with Mickey," Abba says. "There are more plausible reasons for giving up a match. Nick might be sick. Or injured."

I close my eyes. *You don't know the Spences,* I think. The thing I don't understand is why Coach let it happen. He didn't argue. He didn't stand up to Dr. Spence and make sure Mickey got to wrestle. Nick's always bragging that his dad's on our county wrestling board, but that doesn't mean he gets to make the rules. Does it?

"I'm going to help her," I say, without opening my eyes. "I'm going to show the other guys it's okay." I lean my forehead against the cold window to ease my headache. No one warned me being eleven was going to be this complicated.

When we get home, Dalia is sitting in the kitchen, texting and drinking the sloppy green protein shake she always has after field hockey games. Gross.

Abba turns on his laptop. "I've got some work emails," he says. He's holding his headphones up to his ears already. "You okay, Lev?"

I nod because that's what he wants me to do. I boil a hot dog and grab a handful of carrot sticks. I eat as fast as I can. If I'm in the shower before Mom gets back from her study group, she can't practice her counseling stuff on me.

Dalia is already in her pajamas. She must have an early tournament tomorrow. That means Mom will be out all day and it'll be quiet in the house, just me and Abba. I sigh, even though my mouth is full.

Dalia stares at me, acting like she's shocked.

"What?" I mumble around the food in my mouth.

"Number one, you're disgusting. Number two, you're going to choke."

"Aw," I say. "I didn't know you cared." I flash a mouthful of chewed hot dog at her.

Dalia taps her phone with her thumbs. "How'd Mikayla do today?" she asks without looking up.

I wash my food down with water. "The kid she was supposed to wrestle forfeited."

Dalia looks up. "What? On purpose?"

"Maybe. He does things like that."

"You know him?"

I nod. "He's a jerk at school too." I'd tell her more, but Dalia is already walking out of the kitchen.

I stay at the table, finishing my food. I like coming home to a quiet house after a competition. It's lonely, but in a good way. For the last few hours, I've been chasing my friends around the gym, cheering for our teammates, messing around in the bleachers. Even when I'm home, there's so much noise in my brain, I don't have room for talking to people. Besides, how can I talk about today's scrimmage when I don't have a story in my head yet? I don't have the right words to describe what happened. The only way I can figure it out is by writing it in my notebook.

Give It All You've Got,
our team shirts say.
All day we've been running.
Push-ups, squat-jacks
until our arms and legs
shake. Out on the mat
getting cross-faced so hard,
our noses bleed. Sweat
pours from pores
we didn't know we had.
All for a few minutes
to prove we're the best,
a chance they never gave you.

Mr. Van's trying to get me to join the new poetry club at Meadowbrook. A bunch of kids who went to Emerson Elementary thought up the idea. They meet on Wednesdays after school, write poems, eat snacks, and share their work. They're talking about doing a coffeehouse this spring so people can read their poems to an audience. It sounds cool, even though there won't be actual coffee.

"We need your voice, Lev," Mr. Van said when he told me about the group.

But I have practice on Wednesdays.

I look at my new poem. I wouldn't want to share this at school, even with a bunch of sixth-grade poets. At the top of the page, I write *For M.*

I'm still awake when Abba leans into my doorway. Grover pushes past his legs. He's too fat to jump on my bed. He stands there yawning, showing all his teeth.

"Can I have Grover tonight? Please?" Grover is supposed to spend the night in his crate, but Abba knows I sleep better when I have dog company. He scoops both arms under Grover's big belly and lifts him onto my bed forklift-style. Grover puts his chin on my shins.

"What if we didn't go to tournaments and stuff all the time?" I ask. "We could do things at home. We could start Shabbat dinners again. And we could all be in the kitchen cooking together, the way we do on Thanksgiving." I prop up on my elbows.

Abba sits on my bed. He scrubs the side of his head

with a fist. "I forgot to tell you. Dalia has a big tournament on Thanksgiving weekend. Her team is flying to California."

I lie back down and turn on my side. It isn't easy with Grover on my legs. "Are you going with her?" I ask Abba.

"Mom and I decided that I'm staying with you. You have a Thanksgiving tournament too, remember?" He shoves my shoulder, trying to get me to smile.

"We could drive up to New Jersey, see Gran and O.G., and come back on Friday morning. The tournament's not till Saturday."

"They'll be in Florida, visiting O.G.'s sister."

I sigh.

"Maybe one of our neighbors will take pity on us," Abba says.

I turn my head, but just a little, so he knows I'm not totally okay with this. "Can I ask the Hongs?"

"Good idea." Abba kisses the side of my head and says, *"Laila tov."* It's Hebrew for "good night."

Maybe I shouldn't care that my family is going to be in two different places for Thanksgiving, but it's my favorite holiday. It's the day you spend with your family because you're grateful for the food you eat, having a place to live, and people who love you. That's what I'm going to miss, more than turkey and stuffing.

I open my notebook before I go to sleep, but instead of writing, I read what I wrote about last season's qualifier and my match against Nick Spence.

He pushes off, rolls like a log on a river,
with me dancing, trying to stay afloat.

Mr. Van said it was a poem, but for me, it's motivation. I am not going to let that happen again. If Nick and I wrestle at the Thanksgiving tournament, he'll be the one dancing.

That night, I dream about a river. A log has fallen across it, making a bridge. There's someone standing on the other side. He walks to the middle of the log. His face is shadowy, but I hear his voice. He wants me to step onto the bridge so we can wrestle. I put one foot on the log. It's narrow, slippery. And then I'm falling.

CHAPTER 13

Mickey

At Monday's practice, Lev tells me, "You're going to the Thanksgiving tournament."

We're supposed to be practicing stand-ups, but his voice is so bossy, I sit on my heels and give him my Sisterly Death Glare.

I pull out my mouth guard and slip it under the strap of my sports bra. "Coach said it's not for newbies."

Actually, Coach said new Gladiators should only sign up if we want to challenge ourselves. The Eagles' tournament kicks off the whole travel season. Cody told me wrestlers come from all over the East Coast. I don't mention to Lev that I have other plans. There's a "Thriller" rehearsal at Lalita Parsons's house on Saturday. I told Kenna and Lalita I can't be in the act, but maybe I can learn some of the dance, just for fun.

"Exactly, noob," Lev says. "Nick won't be expecting you. Catch him by surprise. He'll have to wrestle you." He clasps his hands together and pulls, like he's going to yank his own arms out of their sockets.

My eyebrows scrunch. "I don't think it works like that."

Does he think being my partner means he can tell me what to do? If Lev were one of my brothers, I'd pop him in the arm.

I put in my mouth guard and move into down-man position. Lev puts all his weight on my back on purpose, to get me riled up. He holds my waist with one hand and my elbow with the other. On the whistle, I kick a leg forward and throw my right arm up. I'm not going to let him push me around. Since this is a drill, Lev lets me break his hold.

"Again!" Coach calls. He's walking around the room, checking everyone's form.

"You need to wrestle," Lev says in my ear as we set up again. "Go sign up with Mrs. Oliver. Show them you're not afraid."

"I'm not afraid," I say around my mouth guard.

"Then you're going."

"I didn't say that."

"Which is it, noob?"

"Sofer. Delgado. Cut the chitchat," Coach says.

I hear a low "Oooo" from somewhere in the room.

Lev widens his eyes at me. I've lived with brothers long enough to know what that look means: *Come on, Mickey.* Usually it's followed by all three of us getting in trouble for doing something we shouldn't, like practicing escapes in the living room.

Lev keeps his grip on me a few seconds longer than he should. He makes me fight my way into the stand-up. I break the hold and turn to glare at him.

He puts his hands up. "Take it out on Spence," he says.

We get out of school early on the Tuesday before Thanksgiving. It's hard to believe I've been at Dickinson Middle long enough that it's time for parent-teacher conferences.

When I get home, there's a box on the front step with my name on it. I carry the package inside, but Cody swoops out of nowhere, grabbing it from my hands.

Until Mom gets back from talking to my teachers, he's in charge. It's the Delgado Next Man Up rule. When the parents are out, oldest kid is in charge. Cody's mad about missing weight training with his team at St. Matt's. I'm not exactly thrilled either, but Mom thinks I'm too young to stay home alone.

"I didn't order anything," Cody says, reading the mailing label.

"Duh. It's got my name on it." I take the box and shake it. Something clunks inside.

Cody pretends to back away. He's grown since he started high school. His jeans barely touch the tops of his sneakers and his T-shirt is too tight. Cody's hair is in between Evan's and mine. Instead of Evan's red curls or my straight brown hair, it's auburn and wavy. You can see the red when he stands in the sun.

Cody says, "It sounds like a bomb. You got any enemies?" He may look mature, but he sure doesn't act like it.

I slice through the tape with a green-painted fingernail.

Under the Bubble Wrap, there's another box. Nestled inside are the brightest hot-pink wrestling shoes I have ever seen.

"Whoa." Cody shields his eyes. "Where are my sunglasses?"

I grin at him without showing my teeth. "This means I don't have to wear your nasty old hand-me-down shoes." I sit on the floor, right there in the hallway, and pop off my loafers. Nothing else in the world feels like wrestling shoes. The soles are thin and flexible from heel to toe, so you can feel your feet and get traction on the mat. I thread the black laces tight along the top of my foot, up to my ankle, then pull the ankle strap closed, covering the knot and bow.

"Is there a note? I bet they're from Dad." I hope they're from Dad.

"Got it." Cody holds up a small card. "They're from Evan. Socks too. They're—uh—loud."

He dangles bright pink knee socks in front of my face. They have a gray hedgehog pattern. The shoes are cool, even though Evan forgot that green is my favorite color. But he remembered I love hedgehogs.

Sometimes I wish Dad were more like Evan. When Evan's in a good mood, he's the best. He buys me and Mom little gifts, flowers for Mom, DC hero buttons for me, just because he knows we'll like them. It mostly makes up for times when he disappears and, like Dad, forgets to call and ask how the first day of school went, or what I'm dressing up as for Halloween, or how it feels to wrestle without Kenna for the first time in my life.

"Here." Cody hands me the card.

I read, " 'You're going to blow up the mat, Mighty Mite. Good luck at your first big tournament!' "

Did Lev tell Evan I'm wrestling on Saturday? My face gets hot.

"What?" Cody asks. He sniffs the box. "Are they poison? Your face is as pink as those shoes."

"Evan thinks I'm going to the Thanksgiving tournament."

Cody lifts an eyebrow. "Aren't you?"

I slump on the floor with one pink shoe in my lap. "There's a dance thing."

Cody breaks into what he thinks is a dance move. I make my face stay completely still.

"You've gotta wrestle, Mickey," he says. "Kicking butt at that tournament is a Delgado tradition."

Since Evan moved out, Cody and I have gotten closer. He used to hate it when Evan was Next Man Up. Evan walked around our house like he was the number one son, and Mom and Dad let him do it. When Nonna was alive, she used to say that at our house, the sun rose and set with Evan's moods. Ever since I can remember, Evan's been like that. When he's happy, I'll find Mom singing show tunes in the kitchen. When Evan's upset, it's like someone pulled all the blinds down and put on emo music.

Cody's not into bossing me around, the way Evan did when he used to babysit us. If Mom's out in the evening, we make breakfast for dinner, French toast and bacon with orange slices. It's delicious. Before he moved out, when Evan was Next Man Up, he told us to make ourselves

PB&J, then disappeared into his room to play video games.

I ask Cody, "Will Evan ever move back home?"

"I doubt it, Mick. You know Dad. He thinks Evan's his best friend or something. Evan gets away with a lot of stuff at Dad's house. No curfew. His own truck."

"The tattoo." It's not fair, the way Mom and Dad treat Evan like he's the rock-star kid of our family just because he was born first. I was born last. What does that make me?

Still, I feel guilty for wishing the good-luck gift were from Dad instead of Evan. I should probably tell Dad I'm wrestling on Saturday. Maybe he'll be so excited, he'll want to come with me. But I'm afraid he'll say I shouldn't go. The Eagles tournament is going to be tough. What if I embarrass myself and him?

CHAPTER 14

Lev

On the last school day before Thanksgiving, we turn in our topics for the language arts mythology project. Everyone's talking about it as we walk into Mr. Van's classroom.

"I'm doing Medusa," Emma Peake says.

Bryan snorts.

Emma frowns. "What's so funny?"

"You just cut off all your hair, and you're doing your project on Medusa. Who's basically all about her hair." Bryan is chuckling.

I like Emma's short haircut. It makes her stand out even more.

Emma puts a hand on her hip and shoots Bryan a look. I'm surprised he doesn't turn to stone. "At least I'm not doing something obvious, like unicorns. Or Superman." She taps Bryan's myth project proposal.

"What's wrong with Superman?"

Emma ignores him and turns to me. "What are you doing?"

"Vampires."

"Dark. I like it."

Mr. Van calls our class to order. Our mythology project will last the rest of second quarter. We have to read and analyze a book related to our subject, create a collage or illustration of our mythological character, and write a poem. Whoa.

"Let me disabuse you all of the notion that this will be a book report," Mr. Van says. "An analysis is a detailed examination of the book's elements. An insightful interpretation." The class groans, but I'm excited about the project. I stop by Mr. Van's desk on the way out of class.

"Mr. Van, I have a theory." I can't wait to tell him. I'm bouncing on my feet.

He smiles through his badger-beard. "I'm all ears, Mr. Sofer."

"I'm comparing vampires to wrestlers."

"Interesting. Tell me more."

"I haven't worked out the details, but it's the way we're always inside. We don't leave the gym until night. We're fast. And we drain our opponents' strength."

I glance at Nick, who's still at his desk, packing up his binder. Mr. Van follows my gaze.

"Fascinating, Lev. I expect you to dig into the roots of the vampire myth. Men's fears are the kernel of that story." As usual, I only have half a clue what he's talking about.

I hurry to make it to PE. Our classes are short because it's a half day, but we still have to change for gym.

When Bryan and I walk out of the locker room, boys and girls are sitting in separate rows on the gym floor. Our ancient PE teacher, Mr. Wilebsky, leans on a metal cart full of basketballs.

"Ugh. I hate basketball," I tell Bryan. I trudge to my spot. We sit alphabetically, which means I'm right in front of Spence. He's wearing sweatpants and a long-sleeved tee under his gym shirt.

"Aren't you hot?" I ask him. I'm sweating already.

"Ask your girlfriend," Spence says. He flips his hair, trying to act cool.

"At least I'm not afraid to wrestle her."

His cheeks turn red. I hope Mickey shows up at the Eagles' tournament this Saturday. When Nick sees her name on the bracket sheet, the look on his face will be epic.

Mr. Wilebsky lines us up behind a row of girls for basketball relays. Nick and I are behind Emma's group. My legs are still aching from last night's conditioning session, but I'm not about to let Nick see me miss a jump shot, especially not in front of Emma.

Emma waves at me from the front of the line. I give her a small nod. One Nick can't see.

The only way I'm going to get through PE today is by goofing off. We're supposed to dribble and pass to the next person in line, but I throw a wild pass on purpose, so Nick has to chase the ball.

"What's your problem, Sofer?"

Want me to make you a list? I think.

Mr. Wilebsky calls me over as the next relay starts.

"I don't want to give you laps, Lev," he says. "Settle down and do the drills right."

"I'd rather take the laps, Coach."

Mr. Wilebsky is bald but makes up for it with out-of-control eyebrows. He raises them at me. "That's not going to earn you a good participation grade for the day." Mr. Wilebsky puts a hand on my shoulder, the way guy teachers do when they want to give you a serious talk. "Everything okay, Lev?" he asks. "Where's that positive attitude?"

I think about telling him how Nick Spence and I are always competing. It doesn't matter if it's wrestling, writing poetry in Mr. Van's class, or stupid basketball drills. I can't get away from him.

"It's wrestling season," I say. "I'm just tired." Which is the truth.

Mr. Wilebsky pats my back. "I've got a lot of respect for wrestlers."

"Can we do a wrestling unit sometime, Coach?" I ask.

"Wish we could. Problem is"—he points to the relay lines—"this is a coed class." His bushy eyebrows move up and down. He doesn't need to spell it out. I have to shake the thought of wrestling Emma Peake out of my head.

I've known some of these girls since kindergarten. Now that we're sixth graders, they're showing up at school wearing lip gloss and body spray. Emma's still my friend, but it's easier talking to Mickey. She's got headgear and braces. She punches me in the arm when I do something wrong. She's one of the guys.

"Get out on the court, Sofer." Mr. Wilebsky pushes me

in the direction of my team, where Nick is bounce-passing the ball to Emma. She takes two steps and aims. The ball goes through the hoop with a perfect swish.

On Thanksgiving morning, I'm still in bed when Bryan texts me. *You up?*

Zzzz.

Coming over. Mom's doing Mad Chef.

The Hongs used to own a restaurant. Bryan's birthday parties are famous for his mother's trays of fried rice, egg rolls, and dumplings. Mrs. Hong's cooking is even better than my O.G.'s, but I hope she's serving plain turkey and mashed potatoes for Thanksgiving.

When I come downstairs, Abba is wearing Mom's cupcake apron. He's in charge of baking bread for our dinner. "Want to help me make the rolls?" he asks.

But the doorbell is ringing. Grover bays at the door, ready to lick the face off whoever comes in our house.

When I let Bryan in, the first thing he does is pet Grover's head. "Hey, fuzzbutt. Long time, no see," he tells the dog.

"Bryan and I are taking Grover for a walk, Abba."

"I like your apron, Mr. S," Bryan says. Abba laughs and flicks some flour at us.

There's an open field with a pond in our neighborhood. Bryan and I like to walk Grover down there. I give Bryan a turn with the leash, because his mom won't let him have a dog. Besides, Grover considers Bryan an honorary member of the Sofer pack.

I explain what happened at the Eagles' scrimmage last

100

weekend. Bryan kicks a stone in his path. "I can't see Spence forfeiting at a tournament. He likes to win too much," he says.

He's right about Spence. Skipping a match at a scrimmage doesn't matter. But if Nick forfeits at a tournament, it counts as a loss on his record for the season.

"There were girls in rec league," I tell Bryan. "Wrestling against them wasn't a big deal. But it is in travel." I lean down to scratch Grover's ears. "What should I do?"

"I don't know. I'm just the dog walker."

We leave the sidewalk and head to the pond. The sun makes a golden light that hits me sideways. I like it out here in the field. After all those hours trapped in school, stuck in the wrestling room, breathing other kids' stale, sweaty air, the autumn wind is fresh. Grover laps water from the pond.

"You want to help this girl, but what's in it for you?" Bryan asks.

I lean down and pat Grover's head. He finds a muddy spot and rolls on his back, squirming and kicking his legs in the air. He's going to need a bath later.

"Nothing. What Nick did to Mickey wasn't fair."

"So you're not helping her because you want to get back at Nick. This has nothing to do with revenge?"

Bryan's words stick with me the whole walk home. He's wrong. I'm not helping Mickey just to prove that Nick Spence is a jerk. That's not who I am.

CHAPTER 15

Mickey

Kenna is not thrilled when I tell her I'm wrestling this weekend. Her family's caught in holiday traffic on the way home from North Carolina, where her grandparents live, so we have to resort to a video chat.

"I was hoping you'd change your mind about the talent show," she says.

"I told you I couldn't do it."

"But you said you'd come to rehearsal tomorrow. I really want you to be there, even if it's just to hang out. Lalita's house is amazing." Kenna's little brother pushes his face between her and the screen, grinning at me. She pushes him away and sighs. "I feel like I only ever see you at school."

Does she think I don't know that? With tournament season starting, Kenna's thrown away her chance to join the Gladiators. She doesn't get to complain about not seeing me, or make me choose between spending time with her and competing. This is her fault.

"You should've thought of that before you quit," I snap. "We would've been spending every weekend together."

Kenna looks at me like I've lost it. "You still don't get it. Wrestling is *your* thing." She frowns at me. "I don't like it anymore. It's not about you."

"I've got to go," I lie. I shut Mom's laptop down, wondering who's going to apologize first, me or Kenna.

On Saturday morning, I'm awake at five a.m., too excited to sleep. Before I pull on my singlet, I study the Gladiator logo on the front. It would be hilarious if we wrestled in feathered helmets, leather skirts, and sandals. I try to picture Lev, Josh, Isaiah, even little Devin and Coach Billy dressed up as historical Roman gladiators. They'd look ridiculous.

"You up, Mikayla?" Mom calls. She walks through my door in her fluffy pink bathrobe. "Cody and I are leaving at quarter to six. Coffee first. Then Cody."

My brother has a wrestling clinic in New Jersey, but when I told Dad I signed up for the Eagles' tournament, he promised he'd take me today.

As soon as Mom shuffles out of my room, I pull Cody's blue Eagles hoodie out of my closet. *Never going to happen,* I tell myself. *Starting today, you're one hundred percent Gladiator.* I ball up Cody's hoodie and shove it in the bottom of my backpack. It's going in the Lost and Found pile at school, where Mom can't rescue it.

Twenty minutes later, Mom, Cody, and I crowd into the kitchen, making lunches and packing our wrestling bags. No one eats. We're not allowed to until after weigh-ins. Cody yawns, barely awake. He'll go back to sleep as soon as he gets in Mom's van. He's got a blanket wrapped around

103

his shoulders like a cape and a pillow stuffed under his sweatshirt.

"Cody the Wonderboy," I say, punching his padded stomach.

"I'm too tired for a sarcastic comeback," he says, swatting my braids. "I'll be in the car, Mom."

"You're sure you're okay?" Mom asks me. "If Dad's not here by six-fifteen—"

I know she's nervous about leaving me alone, but it's only for a few minutes.

"He'll be here," I say. "If not, I'll call Evan. And if Evan doesn't answer, I'll call the Franklins." Mom doesn't know Kenna and I had a fight.

After they leave, it's quiet. I rebraid my hair and check one more time that my headgear, mouth guard, hedgehog knee socks, and pink wrestling shoes are in my bag. I think about packing my stuffie hedgehog too. I'm nervous about today, especially since Dad's coming. Knowing Spike's in my wrestling bag will make me feel better, even if I don't take him out. But I don't want my favorite stuffed animal getting contaminated with sweaty headgear and stinky shoes. I leave Spike behind.

Dad taps his car horn. When I step outside and lock the front door, my breath comes out in a cloudy gush.

"Thanks for coming, Dad," I say, as I get in his beat-up SUV.

"What'd you weigh this morning?" No "Good morning, Mickey." Not even a fist bump.

"Ninety-three point two."

Dad takes a hand off the wheel and makes a "so-so" motion. "You're wrestling ninety-five? Your opponent could have a two-pound advantage on you."

"Nothing I can do about that now."

"Part of the sport," Dad agrees. "Let's hope you don't have to move up a weight class later this season. You never want to be the lightest guy in your bracket."

I don't bother pointing out that I'm not a guy. It's wrestling talk. That's all I get with Dad. He's not the best at talking about school, or friends, or growing up. When he asks me what I'm learning, or how I like sixth grade, our conversations fizzle out. It's easier to talk about the one thing we have in common.

The longer I stay in today's tournament, the more time I get to spend with Dad. Like most competitions, it's double elimination. Lose one match, and you have to wrestle your way back up the bracket, but you can still make it to third place. Lose a second match, and you're out, done for the day.

I can do this without Kenna, I tell myself. The Mickey who needed her best friend and stuffie hedgehog, that's old me. I throw back my shoulders as we step out of the car.

We bump into Lev and his father in the line for weigh-ins. I can't wait to show him my new shoes.

"It's too early in the morning for pink," he kids me.

"They're my secret weapon," I say. "I'm going to stun my opponents with pink power."

Of the hundred or more kids in line, only a few are girls. Everyone's half asleep, shuffling like a robot army.

One by one, wrestlers walk up to the scale, strip down to their singlets, and have their weights written on their upper arms.

When it's my turn, the parent who's in charge of the scales writes *93.2* on my arm. Lev gives me a thumbs-up. His arm says *94.0*. We're both eleven years old, so we'll wrestle in the same bracket: 95 pounds, U12 age group.

It's already loud in the high school gym. Dad sets up his folding chair and pulls out my after-weigh-in breakfast, peanut butter and jelly on a bagel. I spot Nick Spence running up and down the side of the gym in a sweat suit. Make that two sweat suits. He's even wearing a knit cap on his head.

Is he cutting weight? I think.

Some wrestlers do weird stuff to make sure they're in a specific weight class. They chug protein shakes and hit the weight room to get bigger. But usually, they're looking to drop pounds and move into a lower weight class. I've heard stories from Evan and Cody. Kids carrying around spit cups at school to lose water weight. Jogging in double layers of clothing to sweat it off. Cutting weight can be dangerous, so youth wrestlers aren't supposed to do it. But since when has Nick Spence followed the rules?

Before I can tell Lev about Nick, he pulls me toward the trophy table.

"It's your first travel tournament," Lev says, bouncing on his wrestling shoes. He's gotten a haircut. Without his dark wavy hair to cover them, his ears stick out. He has way more freckles than I thought. "Don't you want to know what you're wrestling for?" he asks. There are rows and rows of shiny trophies, each one topped with a golden wrestler boy. "Look at the ones for first place. They're huge!"

Lev leans over the tape that's supposed to stop us from touching the prizes. I pull him back, but he shakes me off. "Don't worry. I won't breathe on them."

"I'll be impressed when I see a trophy with a girl on top," I say. I'm so busy looking at the awards, I don't notice Isaiah leaning over the tape with us. He nods hello.

"Never going to happen," Isaiah says. "No guy wants a trophy with a girl on top." Lev elbows him in the gut, but Isaiah says, "What? It's the truth."

"You think I want a shelf full of trophy boys in my room? No, thank you."

"She's got a point," says Lev.

"Right," Isaiah says. "You complain to the tournament director. He'll say he's not buying girl trophies when there are what—five girls wrestling today?"

I cross my arms over my chest.

"Look," Isaiah says. "I'm sorry about what happened that time at practice. You're a good wrestler, but—"

"I know!" Lev exclaims, grabbing us both by the arm. "We'll invent a trophy with figures you can change! We'll make a million bucks."

I laugh. Isaiah's smiling too. I know Lev's changing the subject, but I like his idea. If I win, why shouldn't I be able to take home a trophy with braids in its hair, long eyelashes, and hot-pink wrestling shoes?

I tell them, "If I win today, I'm going to take my trophy

home, paint its fingernails, and give it pink knee socks to match mine." It actually sounds like fun, a project for me and Kenna. Once we're speaking again. We'll take one of my trophies and give it a makeover.

"We're here to wrestle, not change the universe," Lev says.

"Maybe it needs to change," I mutter, but they don't hear me.

"Where's Josh?" Lev asks Isaiah. I drift away from them, back to Dad.

"Bout sheets are up," he says, holding up his phone. "I took a picture. Eight wrestlers in your bracket. You're on mat four all day."

To anyone who doesn't wrestle, the bracket sheet must look like a complicated math project. Kids' names are listed down the middle, with lines and numbers pointing left and right. I'm the only girl in my age and weight class. I scan the names and only recognize one: Lev Sofer. Nick Spence's name isn't here. Strange.

My first match is number nineteen. Coach Billy walks me onto the mat. "I talked to your opponent's coach," he tells me. "He's a first-year travel wrestler, just like you."

I hear Coach's words, but my ears are buzzing. My fingers and toes prickle like they're going numb. Coach Billy leans down until his nose is practically touching mine. "Dig deep, Mickey. Find that killer instinct."

I nod. "Delgados aren't quitters," I say.

"Atta girl."

It's a close match. We go all three periods. When I win by one takedown, Dad loses his cool. He runs out of the stands, picks me up, and swings me around until my legs fly in the air and we're both laughing.

Dad puts me down and hands me a five-dollar bill.

"You earned a treat. Don't tell your mom," he says. I nod. I'd give him the money back if he'd swing me like that again.

CHAPTER 16

Lev

It's the day of the first tournament. I hear my parents' shower running and pull the covers over my head. I don't open my eyes. If I look at the clock, it's going to say five-thirty. My body feels like I got flattened by a steamroller at last night's practice.

The hall light clicks on. Abba pulls my covers back and shakes me awake.

"Don't wanna get up," I mumble. I had the dream again last night. The shadow-person walked to the middle of the bridge and called to me. He wanted me to wrestle, but when I stepped on the log, I fell, same as before.

I must fall back asleep, because next thing I know, I'm standing on my parents' bathroom scale in underwear and socks. I'm not sure how I got here.

"Ninety-four point six," Abba says. "That's cutting it close. No breakfast until after weigh-ins."

If Mom were here, she'd be brushing her wet hair, splashing it on me, trying to make me laugh, but she and Dalia don't fly home until tomorrow morning.

The rest of the morning is a blur of packing: food for after weigh-ins, peanut butter and jelly sandwich for lunch, apple slices, a few Hershey's Kisses, my headgear and last season's headgear for emergencies, my notebook. I get dressed in layers of red-and-gray Gladiators gear and hope my new singlet doesn't give me armpit wedgies.

Abba sits at the table with a cup of coffee. "Lev, stop bouncing."

I ignore him, plant my hands on the kitchen table and bounce even higher. One of my sandals flies off my sock and hits the back door. Grover woofs.

Abba puts two big hands on my shoulders. "Settle," he says. I look at his scruffy face. His stubble is almost as gray as the hair on his head. Abba leans forward until our foreheads touch. "Save your energy for the tournament."

When we step outside, cold, quiet night touches my face. I hear a long, lonely "hoo."

"Is that an owl?"

Abba nods. "It's a good sign. You're going to wrestle smart today." He rubs the top of my head. "Let's hit the road, Jack."

I toss a pillow and blanket into the back of Abba's SUV. He puts on his favorite band from when he was in high school, Rush. The sound pumps like heat through my muscles.

Why do I love this sport? Who wants to leave the house

before six a.m. on a holiday weekend? It's cold enough to freeze the boogers inside my nose. But later this morning I'll have a great match. I'll feel my opponent hesitate for a second, my instincts will kick in, and the other guy will be on his back, fighting for his life. I'll push down on his chest and slap! The ref's hand will come down and I'll be standing in the center of the mat, victorious.

My first match is against a kid from the Burtonsville Bulldogs. Coach Billy calls me over. "Be aggressive out there," he says. "Take the first shot."

"First shot, best shot." It's one of Coach's favorite sayings.

I jog onto the mat and put on the red ankle cuff. The ref has a matching red cuff on one wrist and a green one on the other. He uses them to tell the judges when a point is scored. Every time he raises his arm with the red cuff, the judges mark down a point for me.

A boy in Burtonsville purple puts on the green cuff, then takes his stance across from me. We shake hands.

"Wrestle!"

Lunge. Knee down, hands out. I grab his leg and pull the Bulldog down, spinning behind him. "Takedown. Two!" the ref yells, and holds up two fingers.

Seconds into the match and I'm sweating. I pull the Bulldog's arm out from under him, forcing him flat to the floor.

"Time!" a voice yells. I don't have time to check in with Coach before the ref sets us up for the second period. I'm top man, my chin hovering above the Bulldog's shoulders.

On the whistle, I move. Almost without thinking, I sink a half nelson, sliding an arm through the kid's elbow and behind his head. I roll the boy over. He pants and groans, kicks and bucks. I hold on. The ref is belly down on the mat next to us. I catch his eye for a second as he checks the Bulldog's shoulders. Slap! The ref's hand hits the mat.

It's over.

"That's the killer instinct I want to see," Coach Billy says, grabbing me around the shoulders. First match of the season, and I pinned my guy. I've got this. I know I'm good enough to make it to States.

CHAPTER 17

Mickey

Lev finds me in the hallway, studying the updated bracket sheets. There's an *F* for *Fall* next to his name. Pinning a guy in your first match of the season. I bet that feels awesome.

"How'd you do?" he asks, trying to see around me.

"I won."

"You did? You don't sound happy about it."

I point to my next match on the bracket sheet, number fifty-three. Lev's name is right under mine.

"Oh," he says. "That stinks."

"You'd better not go easy on me just because you're my partner. Pretend you've never seen me before in your life."

"Quit worrying. Josh and I have wrestled at tournaments plenty of times."

"I thought you'd be all about the Fearsome Threesome today," I say as we walk back to the gym. Lev tilts his head toward the cafeteria. Josh and Isaiah are in line, waiting for hot dogs, chili, and donuts. Once weigh-ins are over, wrestlers love their junk food.

A kid passes us. The slogan on his T-shirt says *On the Mat, Beneath the Light, That's Where Real Men Come to Fight.*

"Give me a Sharpie," I say. "I need to fix that shirt. It should say *That's Where Women Come to Fight.*"

"You can have this." Lev pulls a pen out of his special notebook.

"You'd give me the pen from your journal? I'm honored."

He grimaces. "It is not a journal. It is a notebook. Besides, I agree with you. Coach Billy says wrestling is for anyone tough enough to step on the mat."

"Then he's full of it." I take a long drink from my water bottle.

"You don't think that's true?"

"If you're a boy. I have to work twice as hard as everybody else in the practice room."

The other day at lunch, Lalita asked me if I like Lev, and not just as a partner. "Is he boyfriend material?" she wanted to know. She shivered, which made her hair bow shake.

Kenna scowled at her. "Do we have to talk about boys?"

"Exactly," I said. "We're eleven."

"I'm not eleven," Lalita said. "I turned twelve in October." She leaned across the table and told us in a low voice, "My sister got her period when she was twelve." Lalita shivered again and smiled with her electric blue braces showing, like this was the most exciting news ever.

I guess Lalita might call Lev cute, but I think he was cuter with long hair. He looks younger and goofier with short hair and those funny ears. I think it makes me like him even more. As a friend.

"Are there any Eagles in our bracket?" I ask Lev.

"Spence is here today, but I don't see his name." He scratches his short hair where his headgear made a cowlick. "He's supposed to be wrestling ninety-five, like us."

In the hall, a vendor is selling Maryland State Wrestling hoodies. I spot Nick Spence in line with his little sister. Her pink T-shirt is exactly like one I had before I started wrestling: *Wrestler's Sister: Stay on My Good Side.*

Nick glares at us as we walk by.

"I like your wrestling shoes. Pink is my favorite color," his sister says to me. Her blond hair is in two French braids, just like mine. Nick tries to pull her away, but she tells me, "I'm going to wrestle like my brother."

"In your dreams, Anna," Nick says to her, but he's smiling.

I get a good look at the number written on Nick's arm before we go back to the gym.

"Did you see that, Lev?" I ask. "Eighty-nine point three."

I was right. This morning, Nick was trying to sweat off a couple of extra ounces before weigh-ins.

"Spence is cutting weight," I say. "He's wrestling in the ninety-pound weight class."

"Why would he do that?" Lev looks confused, but I know exactly what's going on.

"So he doesn't have to wrestle me."

I don't say anything to Dad, but I think about Nick Spence the rest of the day.

I was at a dual meet with Cody once, when he was on the Eagles. We were in the stands watching a match when one of the older boys went into convulsions. His dad laid him flat on the bleachers. Dr. Spence ran up the steps with another doctor, a mom from the opposing team. EMTs had to take the kid out on a stretcher. Mom told me later, he'd been cutting weight. The convulsions happened because all the fluids and chemicals in his body were out of whack. It was scary. I will never cut weight. Mom says it's not healthy for me if I want to, as she puts it, "develop." Sometimes Mom reminds me of Lalita Parsons.

After Lev and I warm up, he finds Coach and I get my dad. Dad's going to coach me so Lev can have Billy the Kid in his corner.

I tuck my braids into my cap and put on my headgear and mouth guard. I back into Dad's chest like I've seen Evan and Cody do a million times. He wraps his arms around my shoulders, lifting me off the ground with a squeeze that stretches my muscles.

"Go get 'em," he says.

I put on the green ankle cuff, my lucky color, praying I make it to the end of the match without getting pinned. Lev wraps the red cuff around his ankle. Even though I've already won a match today, I think, *I'm going to freeze. I'm going to forget how to do this.*

The voices in the crowd go fuzzy as I take the mat. Then the whistle blows, and Lev and I are grappling. My hands grip his arms, pushing him back without letting him loose. He puts a palm on my forehead, then pulls my head down. When I react, he takes a shot and grabs me behind the knees, his head in my middle. Then my feet are off the ground. I land hard on my butt. I scramble to turn and base up.

"Two!" the ref shouts. I see his red cuff flash above me. Lev's winning already.

Once I'm in down position, I tuck up and stay there. Lev tries to force my shins apart with his knees and flatten me out on my stomach, but I won't let him.

A faraway voice says, "Time!" The ref signals us to get up.

I'm panting when I get to Dad's corner. He smiles and cups a hand behind my head. "You're putting up a great fight out there. That's your partner?"

I nod.

"He's a good wrestler."

I don't last the full three periods. Early into the third, my stomach's pressed to the floor. Lev has his elbow in my back. I can't let him pin me, but the score is 15–0, enough for Lev to earn a technical fall. The ref stops the match. When he raises Lev's hand in the air, I'm too embarrassed to look at him.

After I shake hands with Lev and Coach Billy, I jog to my dad's corner of the mat.

"Did he have to tech me?" I ask.

I must sound like I'm whining. Dad's jaw tightens. He is not happy with me. "You went defensive," he says. "Next time, take a shot instead of tucking up and stalling." Dad hands me a tissue. "No crying on the mat, Mikayla. Go clean up and get back out there."

I splash water on my face in the girls' room. I haven't

lost a match in almost a year. Last time a kid beat me this bad, Kenna was the one who found me in the bathroom. She rubbed my back and handed me tissues until I stopped crying. Now she's having fun at Lalita Parsons's amazing house, and I'm hiding in a high school girls' room.

I dab cold water on my eyes one more time before going back to the gym. Then I climb to the top of an empty bleacher with a book and try to forget about getting creamed.

"Hey, Mickey. Nice view." Lev pulls himself up to sit next to me.

"I'm not speaking to you."

"Why?" He looks surprised. Lev holds out an open pack of Twizzlers. "Because I beat you?"

"Teched me. I didn't even score one point."

"At least it wasn't a pin," he says. He pulls out one red twist of candy and chomps it. "You told me not to go easy on you."

I ignore him and open my book.

"You're upset."

"How'd you guess?"

He pokes me in the chin. "You do this thing with your face when you're mad. You push your chin out."

I'm not sure I like that Lev knows this about me.

"Hey, it's your first tournament," he says. "Stay mad at me if you have to, but take it out on your next guy. You don't want to be done for the day."

I grimace at him. My lips peel back from my braces. "Mad enough for you?"

"It's a start." He holds out the Twizzlers again. "Best

119

candy for wrestling," he says, pulling another twist out of the pack with his teeth.

"You're gross, you know that?"

"That's what all the girls say. And by 'all the girls,' I mean my sister."

I laugh and take a Twizzler. It's sweet and just chewy enough to make me feel better.

Later, when I lose another match, Coach Billy tries to cheer me up.

"You won one. Not bad for your first time out," he says. He puts his hand up for a high five. I slap it but don't give it much oomph. Coach peers into my face. "Where's the firecracker I see at practice?" he asks. "You did a good job, Mickey. For your first tournament, you killed it."

Dad's not into fake enthusiasm. He's used to being with Evan and Cody. They always bring home trophies. I can tell he's disappointed when we leave the tournament early. He's quiet as we walk out of the building.

"I heard what that last kid said when he was walking off the mat," Dad says. He pulls a ski cap over his ears. They're puffy and messed up from wrestling in high school, and now from his jujitsu gym.

"I didn't hear anything. What'd he say?"

"Some garbage about how the match was close because he didn't want to hurt a girl." Dad opens the door for me. Outside, the sun is already setting. "You wrestled with a lot of heart today, Mickey. Boys like that, they're making excuses. They don't want to look bad in front of their friends. It's a guy thing."

"I know, Dad. If I win, they say they went easy on me. If I lose, I'm not good enough to wrestle them."

"I admit, I wasn't sure moving you up to travel was a good idea. You've shown me different. You're a winner to me." Dad wraps an arm around my shoulders and squishes me against his side. As we get in the car, he says, "Donuts on the way home?"

"Really? Evan and Cody only get donuts when they win."

"Can't a dad take it easy on his only daughter?" He laughs.

This is what I wanted. Me and Dad, talking like we see each other every day.

CHAPTER 18

Lev

I feel bad about beating Mickey like that at her first tournament. Teching her felt like I was showing off. But she told me not take it easy on her.

I ended up taking third place. Not bad for my first competition of the season. I'm on the path to States.

December is a blur. We have Gladiators practice three nights a week, dual meets and tournaments every weekend. Bryan knows the next few weeks are all about mat time, adding wins to my record, learning from my losses. When I have a free afternoon, we work on our mythology projects together. Other than that, we don't see each other outside of school, but Bryan says he's used to it.

One night, after warm-ups, Coach Billy calls us to the center of the mat for a demonstration. "We're doing an advanced spin drill, men," he says.

Mickey elbows me. "Men?"

I elbow her back. "Shut up. Listen."

We've always done spin drills the same way. Bottom man stays in referee's position while the top wrestler moves from his legs, his chest skimming his partner's back as he spins.

Coach Billy tries to explain the new drill, but kids keep raising their hands and asking questions. Coach's face is turning red. He's going to blow any second. Then Isaiah's mom comes up and puts a hand on Billy the Kid's elbow. I widen my eyes at Isaiah. His mom is fearless.

"Coach?" she says. "Why don't you ask for two volunteers to demonstrate?"

Coach Billy is shocked that she interrupted him, but he nods. "Good idea."

I raise my hand to volunteer. When Coach points at me, I grab Josh and we walk to the center of the circle.

"Josh, Lev, you're at neutral," Coach Billy says. "We're going to do this at half speed. Lev, start with a single leg takedown."

Josh lets me shoot and grab his right knee.

"Normally, Lev trips Josh's standing foot with his attacking leg," Coach Billy says. It feels strange to move this slow. "You gonna let Sofer have that, Josh?" Coach shouts. "Hop those legs back, hard. Lev's head'll come down. Now push down on his shoulders and sprawl, feet apart."

Josh spins around me to get the takedown. Coach doesn't even have to explain it to him.

"Did everyone see that? That was perfect! Feet apart. Never on your knees. You can't move from your knees. Let's go again. This time, Lev, you're moving too. When

Josh tries to spin, match his motion and keep your head in his gut."

Josh and I smile at each other. We set in neutral again. "We're doing it for real this time. Match speed," Coach tells us.

I grab the leg. Josh hops back in a sprawl. He slaps two palms hard against my shoulders. My head comes up, crack, against his chin.

"Whoa," Coach calls, putting a hand on Josh's back. "Easy, you two. We're demonstrating."

I sit on my heels. That's when I see blood dripping from Josh's mouth. He covers his chin and lips with his hand.

Coach Billy kneels down in front of Josh. "Let me see."

I lean forward. "What happened?" My eyes prickle.

Josh moves his hand away. "Bit my tongue," he mumbles.

"Andrea!" Coach calls. Mrs. Oliver comes out on the mat with a first-aid kit. The room is quiet, except for a few whispers. "Blood time," Coach says, spinning a finger in the air, the way refs do when a wrestler is injured. "Partner up, everyone. Sit-ups, mountain climbers, push-ups. Find a spot. Go."

Isaiah and Mickey pull me out to the hallway.

"Where are we going? Is Josh okay?"

"My mom's a nurse," Isaiah says. "She'll take care of him."

"Why are we out here? I have to see if he's okay."

"There's blood in your hair," Mickey says. "You need to rinse it off. You clocked him pretty hard."

"Yeah," Isaiah says. "Your skull is like an anvil."

I touch the top of my head. It's sore where I hit Josh's chin. When I look at my fingers, I see blood.

"Stop freaking out," Mickey says. She puts an arm around my shoulders. "I bit my tongue one time when I was wrestling with my brothers. Tongues can bleed a lot, even from a little cut."

They help me wash up in the bathroom sink. Isaiah cracks a joke about Mickey being in the boys' room, but it's not funny. I didn't mean to hurt Josh. When he slapped my shoulders, my head popped up. It was automatic.

Josh sits out the rest of practice, holding paper towels to his mouth. "I'm fine," he tells me. "Got all my teeth, see?"

But when I get home that night, I can't sleep. Abba must see that my light is on. He comes in and sits on my bed.

"What is it?"

"I've been having nightmares."

"You want to talk about it?"

I put my head back on the pillow and close my eyes. "It's about a river. I have to walk across a log bridge. There's someone at the other end and he wants me to wrestle, but the log isn't that wide, and the water's far below." I feel my heart pounding, remembering the dream.

"Then what?" Abba asks. "Do you wrestle?"

I shake my head. "I fall."

"Scooch over," Abba says. He lies down next to me and

turns out the bedside light. "Mrs. Oliver told me what happened at practice. How's your head?"

I rub the spot where my skull met Josh's chin. "Sore."

"Josh will be fine. No spicy food for a couple of days."

"Not funny, Abba."

"Go to sleep. It's going to be fine."

CHAPTER 19

Mickey

Evan and Cody only want one thing for Christmas: to watch the big UFC fight on pay-per-view.

Me? I'm asking for hip-hop lessons with Lalita and Kenna once wrestling season is over. After Kenna and I apologized to each other, we agreed that we need to plan something fun we can do together now that she's not wrestling. And since hip-hop classes were Lalita's idea, the three of us are signing up together.

Of course, Mom got super excited when I told her what I wanted. "Maybe I'll get to be a theater mom after all," she said. No, thank you.

Mom is not so happy with Evan and Cody's idea. "Kick-boxing. Exactly what we need to get in the Christmas spirit," she complains. "Wouldn't you rather watch *The Sound of Music*?"

Mom's sarcasm is wasted on Cody's peanut brain. "UFC *is* in the Christmas spirit," he says. "Jesus kicks Judas's butt in a mixed martial arts showdown."

I slap my palm to my forehead. Cody gives new meaning

to the word *inappropriate*. Anything that pops into his head pops right out of his mouth.

"Wrong holiday," I say. "The Jesus/Judas smackdown is Easter."

"You two need remedial Sunday school," Mom says. She lifts a Santa dressed in a wrestling singlet and headgear out of the ornament box. We're religious, but this time of year, that religion is wrestling. We spend more time at tournaments than we do at church.

No surprise, Dad takes Evan and Cody's side. I never realized it before, but they are the Delgado family's Fearsome Threesome, and I want in.

"I think we should do it," Dad says when he picks Cody up for a dual meet. "If you're okay with having the party here, I'll handle the rest. Food. Everything. I'll ask Billy and some of the Gladiators dads. The boys can invite their teammates." Dad is convinced that the kids we know from wrestling are a good influence on us. I guess he's never seen Cody and his St. Matt's teammates attack a pizza. Mom says they should change the team mascot to a vulture.

"What about me?" I ask. My brothers aren't the only ones with wrestling friends. But my question gets lost in Dad and Cody's whirlwind of plans for the party.

On Christmas Day, we're supposed to be relaxed and happy, singing Christmas carols and opening gifts, but Evan's wearing his I'm-too-old-for-this face. He spends most of the day hunched over his phone. I haven't seen him lately.

Evan's supposed to bring up his grades this semester, to impress colleges with his GPA, not just his wrestling record. He's had some interest from college scouts, but nothing he can count on. No one's promising my brother a scholarship. I hear my parents fight about it over the phone sometimes. Dad says Mom babies Evan and that if she keeps emailing his teachers, stepping in to fix things, he'll never grow up.

After Christmas cookies and hot chocolate, Dad, Evan, and Cody clear the table so they have room to plan a menu for Fight Night. I linger in the kitchen, dunking Christmas cookies in my hot chocolate. Cody knows I'm eavesdropping.

"Come on, Mikayla," he says, pulling out a chair for me. "Admit it. You want to watch the fight."

"Only because girls are the main event," I say. The champ is a former Olympic women's wrestler who's defending her MMA title.

Cody leans close to me. "It's going to be *bloody*."

I put my hand over his face and push him away. "I want to invite a friend too."

"As long as you leave us guys alone while you do your makeovers." Cody flutters his eyelashes at me.

I try to grab him in a headlock, but Cody slips away.

"Shrimp," he calls me under his breath. It's so annoying when Evan comes home. Cody starts showing off, acting like his old jerky self. I like it better when he thinks he's the big brother. When he's Next Man Up, he's nicer to me.

"Who do you have in mind, Mikayla?" Dad asks.

"Lev Sofer." I ignore Cody's kissing noises. "Stop being gross, Cody. He's my *partner*."

For the past two months, I've spent most of my time with the Gladiators. Sixth grade will be halfway over in a few weeks, and I know Lev better than the kids at Dickinson Middle. I think about inviting Kenna too. But she's been spending all her free time with Lalita lately. Besides, she wouldn't be interested in staying up past eleven to watch kickboxing.

Evan tells Dad, "Lev's a nice kid. He's been a good partner to Mickey. Right, Mighty Mite?"

"Mickey's got a boyfriend," Cody teases. I should leap out of my seat and chase him up the stairs, but it's Christmas, so I settle for giving him the Sisterly Death Glare.

CHAPTER 20

Lev

I love winter break. I love keeping my eyes closed and listening to the sounds of the house. There's no school, no tournament, no reason to get up.

I hear Mom feeding Grover breakfast. His nails skitter on the kitchen tiles. He snorts as he swallows his food. The coffeepot gurgles.

Through my eyelids, I can tell the light is changing from sunrise to full-on morning. Today, there are no wrestling bags or field hockey sticks to pack. No lunches or jugs of water to get ready. No sweat-stinking uniforms or singlets we forgot to wash.

I wander downstairs, following the scent of pancakes. Grover snuffles over and gives me good-morning licks. Mom is at the stove. She turns to smile at me. "Morning."

"You're making pancakes. I'm happy," I say, wrapping my arms around her middle.

"Because you slept."

"Because pancakes." I pull the comics out of the newspaper. Watching Mom do normal parent stuff—cooking a hot breakfast instead of getting up early to help me pack—I wonder what our family would be like if Dalia and I didn't do sports all the time. Maybe we'd take more walks down to the frog pond together, or play card games like Uno every Saturday night, or start inviting people for Shabbat dinner again.

"The sun feels nice," I say, looking out the back door.

"Mmm-hmm."

"Wrestlers are like vampires. If we go in the sun, we shrivel up and lose all our strength."

"And the drinking-blood thing?" Mom flips a pancake.

I don't want to think about that. "I'm writing a poem for my mythology project. It's just a draft." If I still like it by the end of break, I'm going to show my poem to Mr. Van.

Mom puts a stack of pancakes in front of me. "What are you up to today?"

"Dalia said she'd help me pick out a Hanukkah present for Evan."

Mom's eyebrows shoot up like twin rockets.

"I know he's not Jewish, but he took me out for ice cream for my birthday, remember? I owe him one."

It happened before school started. Dalia thought I was hijacking their date, but Evan said he couldn't enjoy eating ice cream if they left me home on my birthday. He bought enough for my parents and insisted we bring it back to the house. Mom called it an impromptu party. When the ice cream was gone, Evan pulled me into the family room, grabbed me behind the leg with his scruffy red head in my side, and lifted me into a fireman's carry. Grover got so excited, he actually woofed.

"No wrestling in the house," Mom said. "Grover doesn't like it." But she was laughing.

After breakfast, my sister and I sit in Abba's basement office. We argue over who gets the leather desk chair and who sits in the kiddie chair from Dalia's old tea party table. It isn't that I'm afraid of her. I could take Dalia in a fight. But she has me beat when it comes to stubbornness. If I insist on having the good chair, Dalia will leave me to pick Evan's present by myself.

We used to get along better, even after she started field hockey. Then one day, when I'd been wrestling for a while, she was chasing me in the backyard, tickling me. I told her to stop, but she wouldn't. I turned around so fast, she didn't know she was supposed to get out of my way. I shot a foot behind her ankle, a perfect wrestling trip. Dalia toppled straight back like a falling tree. Her head hit the ground. Not very hard, but Dalia didn't talk to me for three days, not until Abba made her say she forgave me. I don't think she ever trusted me after that.

I pull the kiddie chair closer and sit on my knees so I can see the screen. Dalia scrolls through wrestling T-shirts.

"What are you getting Evan?" I ask.

"None of your business."

"It's just a question."

Dalia sighs. "Look. I'm glad you and Evan are friendly,

but he's my boyfriend. Some things between us are private."

My ears feel like they're on fire. I wish I still had my long hair to cover them. "Forget it," I say. "I'll ask Mom to take me to the mall."

Dalia rolls her eyes. "You want to get Evan something he likes, don't you? Mom will talk you into a self-help book, *Surviving Your First Year of College,* something she thinks is useful."

I shrug. "I guess."

"What about this one?"

She points to a shirt on the screen. It's light gray, with dark red writing. *"Tell me what you see when your face hits the mat,"* I read. "Sounds brutal."

"That's why he'll like it. He's always talking about the rush he gets when he knows he's got a kid beat."

"He is?" My legs are cramping. I catch myself from falling off the chair.

Dalia sighs again but gives me a hand up. "Evan says he can feel it when his opponent gives up. It's like in field hockey, when I see a lane open up for a breakaway." Dalia glances at her pinging cell phone. I'd better pick a shirt before she disappears.

"You're sure he'll like it?"

"I know he will, Lev. Honestly, he'd like anything from you. Evan likes being your hero."

But when I read the shirt, I hear Spence's voice saying, *I'm going to crush you.* Evan's not like that, talking smack and messing with people's heads before a match. Coach says we have to have the killer instinct, to dominate our opponents on the mat, but we're also supposed to protect them. When we practice lifts, Coach reminds us it's our job to make sure the other guy lands safely on the mat.

"Sure," I tell Dalia. "That one." But I can't shake the thought of Josh covering his bleeding mouth.

Over winter break, Gladiators practice is optional. My parents are having a date night, so Dalia drives me. I can tell she's mad because she doesn't turn on her music when we get in the car. She's always mad lately.

A couple of days ago, Dalia tried to skip out on the first night of Hanukkah. I was like, "Dalia, presents," and she told me to grow up.

She wanted to go to a movie with some girls from her club team. When Abba said no, we were celebrating Hanukkah as a family, Dalia threw a fit.

"Latkes are disgusting," she said. "My hair reeks of oil and onions for days."

Now, as she turns the car out of our neighborhood, I ask, "Do you like field hockey more than you like us?"

She keeps her eyes on the road. "What are you talking about?"

The other night, when I lit the menorah with Mom and Abba, Dalia sat at the table with her arms crossed and her lips in a tight line. Her eyes looked like she wanted to shoot lasers into the empty air.

"It was weird saying the Shehecheyanu without you," I tell her. "We always say the first-night prayer together."

"You're too young to understand," she says. It's one of her favorite sayings, but this time, maybe because we're alone in the car, she explains. "When I started high school, being on the field hockey team made everything better. I had friends before classes started. Upperclassmen from the team looked out for me." She slows the car at a red light and turns to look at me. "You'll see when you wrestle in high school."

"What if I decide not to?"

It's the first time I'm saying the thought out loud. Right away, I want to take it back. I'm a wrestler. I've been a wrestler since I was seven years old.

"Why would you quit?" Dalia asks. "Evan says you're really good."

"He does?"

"All the summer camps you've done, moving up to the travel team. It's all prep for high school. That's when the real competition starts."

"Coach Billy says that too."

The light changes. The car is quiet and I think Dalia's done talking to me until she asks, "Don't you like wrestling anymore?"

"I like practice—drilling with my friends. I like the kids on the team." I like Mickey. She's a good partner, even if she is a noob. But ever since Josh and I knocked into each other at practice, live wrestling isn't fun.

"It's not that kid from the Eagles, is it?" she asks. "Don't let him mess with you. Evan says he's still giving Mickey a hard time."

In all the tournaments we've gone to this season, if Nick's there, he finds a way to avoid wrestling Mickey. Sometimes I sit in the stands and watch her matches. The way kids and parents talk about her is changing. Since the first couple of competitions, she's been getting better, winning more close matches. People are impressed. Strangers cheer for her, because she's a girl and she's good. Coach says Mickey's going to place at a tournament any day now.

A tow truck passes. Its flashing yellow lights make Dalia's face look almost soft.

"I thought you wanted to make States," she says.

"What if I don't qualify again this year? How am I going to be a state champ like Evan?"

Maybe she doesn't know what it's like, being a boy in middle school, always trying to measure up to the other guys who brag about football and lacrosse, who'd rather get the girls to flirt with them than get good grades.

"Careful what you wish for," Dalia says. Does she try to sound like a parent, or does it just come naturally for older sisters?

"What do you mean?"

"Evan made state champ in eighth grade, and he's been trying to live up to himself ever since, trying to prove he's still the best. I think it makes him unhappy."

I don't get it. How could being state champ make anyone unhappy?

"You're eleven, Lev. You've got plenty of time to make it to the state tournament. If you don't earn a spot this year, you'll keep trying."

Dalia pulls up to the back door of the school where we practice. Instead of driving away, she rolls down the window. "Stop worrying so much. Have fun. Wrestle hard." She smiles. It's the second time this week my sister has smiled at me.

CHAPTER 21

Mickey

Too soon, winter break is over and we're back at school. The first weekend in January is Fight Night, our big Delgado UFC party. There's a Beginning Champions tournament in New Jersey that same Saturday. I want to stay home and help get ready for the party, but Coach Billy says this tournament is perfect for me. Only first- and second-year travel wrestlers can compete.

"You're going to clean up, Delgado," he says, putting out his hand for a fist bump. "I want to see you there on Saturday."

Mom drives me to New Jersey for the tournament because Dad needs to clean the house and make food for the party. I hope Evan and Cody are helping him. There are wrestling shoes, old socks, and sweaty headgear strewn all over our house.

At the tournament, I pin my first kid right away. My second bout is against a boy who, I can tell, is weirded out about wrestling me. His holds are so loose, I get some easy escapes and rack up points on him.

Two wins and a small bracket means I'm already in the

championship round, against a kid from the Timberwolves, Trent Wheeler. This could be it. My first chance all season to get a first-place win.

Before the match, Coach Billy calls me over.

"You ever wrestled a blind kid before?" he asks.

I haven't, but I've seen Evan and Cody compete against all kinds of wrestlers.

"There's not much difference, especially when you're down on the mat," Coach says. "The only rule is to maintain contact. The ref will show you what to do."

I kneel down and put on the red cuff. Two Timberwolves kids step onto the mat. One's got his headgear on, ready to wrestle. His teammate holds his elbow and walks him to the center, then helps him put the green cuff on. When we're set across from each other, the boy puts out his hands, one palm up and one palm down.

"Touch up," the ref says. I grasp the Timberwolf's hands, palm to palm. "If you break contact, I'll stop the match and we reset. Understand?"

We both say yes.

It's a close match. We grapple all through first period, with no one getting the advantage. My mind is so focused on wrestling, I let go a couple of times by accident. The ref blows his whistle, walks my opponent back to the center of the mat, and starts us again.

There's still no score at the start of the third period. It's my turn to be in the down position. This kid is tough, but somehow I'm able to get out, spin behind him, and get a reversal. Those are the only two points scored in the whole match.

We meet in the center one more time to shake hands. "Good match!" I say, as I lead him back to his coach.

"The other kids I wrestled today? They didn't take me seriously." He grins. "I made 'em regret it. This *was* a good match. Thanks, man."

"You know I'm a girl, right?"

"Yeah, I figured that out." His smile makes me laugh.

I clap him on the back. "See ya!"

When I head back to the stands, Mom gives me a gigantic squeeze. Then Mrs. Oliver hugs me. "We're very proud of you, Mickey!" she says. Isaiah's mom is so nice. I'm glad we have a huggy, sweet team mom like her to balance out Coach Billy.

Other Gladiators parents give me high fives or pat me on the back and say, "Great match, Mickey." They all know me. How did that happen? Even Devin comes running over. He leaps up and I catch him in a hug.

Mom and I blast music on the drive home. I rock out, waving my first-place trophy.

"I'm trying to drive, here." Mom laughs.

I stick my trophy between the seats and tap Mom's arm with it. In a deep voice, I say, "Trophy Boy wants a donut." I'm not sure she knows about Dad's donut tradition with Evan and Cody. It started when Evan joined the Eagles. If a Delgado earns third place or better at a tournament, there will be donuts. No questions asked.

Mom doesn't complain that donuts are a Dad thing. She smiles and says, "You earned it."

I run in the store and look for the gooiest, most icing-covered donuts on the shelf. I'm going to eat at least one in the car. I pick out a blueberry cake donut for Mom, plus a box of Munchkins for the party.

There's no way I'm waiting until tonight to tell Lev my news. I text him a picture of my trophy as we drive home. He's at a tournament in Pennsylvania with the more experienced Gladiators.

No Trophy Girl? ☺ *1st Place* ☺*!* he texts back.

Not complaining, I type. *Help me paint his toes later.*

It's late, almost nine o'clock, when people start coming over. Cody's friends from St. Matt's arrive first. Then a couple of fathers from the Gladiators. When Coach Billy comes in, he says, "There's the champ!" He pretends to put a hand out for me to shake, then catches me in a tie-up. "Big win today, Delgado. I talked to the Timberwolves coach. That kid Trent? Coach says he's tough as nails."

I just nod. It's bizarre seeing my wrestling coach in my house. I keep expecting him to shout, *Drop and give me twenty!*

Finally, Lev, his sister, and Mr. Sofer are here. Even in his jeans and *Gladiators Dad* polo shirt, Mr. Sofer looks dressed up. He wears loafers instead of sneakers, and his hair is gelled back. Lev said he works for the government. The way he stands, back straight and shoulders high, I wonder if he's ex-military, like my dad.

"Thanks for inviting me, Mr. Delgado," Lev says.

I've only ever seen Lev in wrestling gear. He's dressed up for our party too, khakis and a green-and-blue-striped sweater. He's got a lumpy grocery bag under his arm.

Dalia comes in behind him. Lev says they don't get along, but I think she looks friendly. When Evan whisks her away to meet Mom, Lev follows me down the hall.

"I've never met your sister before. She's pretty."

"She doesn't usually look that nice. She's more sporty."

"You do *not* look alike." Dalia doesn't have Lev's freckles, his sticking-out ears, or his round face. Her hair is dark brown, long, and straight, not wavy like his.

"Thanks a lot, noob." Lev shoves my arm.

When we get to the kitchen, Cody and his friends are devouring Dad's chili and wings. The boys put Doritos into paper bowls, ladle scoops of chili on top, and smother it with shredded cheese.

"I can't watch," Mom says. Two seconds later she's yelling at Cody, "Spoons! We have spoons. Chili is not finger food, you animals." Cody licks his fingers at Mom, but he grabs a handful of plastic spoons to pass around. Mom and Dalia look at each other and roll their eyes.

I watch Lev and Evan together as they move extra chairs into the family room, near the TV. I can tell they're good friends. Evan catches Lev in a headlock and knuckles his skull until they're both smiling. He doesn't wrestle like that with Cody. Cody gets angry and stalks out of the room when he can't beat Evan. And Evan never, ever lets Cody win.

Lev and I sit cross-legged on the family room floor. The

dads, my brothers, and their friends, including Dalia, took all the good seats.

Lev asks, "Do guys have to do mixed martial arts if they want to wrestle after college? I don't want somebody elbowing my head."

"Wrestlers do well in mixed martial arts," Evan says. "Of course, you've got to learn how to box." I notice him sneaking a sideways glance at Dad. "There's a gym not far from here. I'm thinking about checking it out."

The happy look on Dad's face snaps shut. "Forget it, Evan. Focus on school and wrestling. You still have to get into college. You don't have time for MMA."

Evan frowns at the plate of pizza on his lap. "I'm almost eighteen. It's not up to you."

"Guess you're planning on working your own way through college, then."

The room gets quiet. Why do they have to argue when we have people over?

Evan stands. His shoulders are scooped forward like he wants to reach out and grab Dad, wrestle him to the ground. Dalia puts a hand on his back and he sits.

Mom stands on the step between the kitchen and the family room. "I don't want you boys doing MMA," she says. "At least in wrestling, the point is submission, not injury."

Evan shakes his head. "That's not true. When you've got an arm bar on a guy, you're trying to hurt him, to break his will so he wants to give up and get the match over with."

Lev stares at Evan. I need to get us out of here before

Dad and Evan start arguing for real. I scoot across the carpet, closer to him.

"Let's get the trophy."

"It's with my coat."

We find the pile of jackets in Mom's bedroom and dig out Lev's grocery bag. When we texted each other this afternoon, Lev said I shouldn't mess with my Beginning Champions trophy, since it's from my first tournament win as a Gladiator. He offered to bring one of his old trophies for our project. It's about ten inches tall, with a gold wrestler on top.

"It's from rec league," he says. "When I was nine."

"Third place. Not bad!"

"What's the plan?"

"Pink shoes, for sure. Maybe the singlet too. I've got nail polish."

"What about his hair?"

"*Her* hair?"

"We could add a ponytail. Do you have hair-colored nail polish?"

"Let's use a Sharpie. Put on your coat."

Lev looks confused. Clearly, he is not used to doing non-parent-approved crafts. "We'll do it in the garage. No one will notice. They're too busy watching the fights. Also, if we work out there, the nail polish smell won't give us away."

Lev grins. "I had no idea you were an evil mastermind."

I give him a low bow.

We take the Sharpie and some hot-pink polish and head out to the garage. It's so cold, my teeth chatter.

145

"Would it bother you if Evan did MMA?" Lev asks. He watches me paint polish over the trophy's gold singlet and feet. I brush on pink knee socks too, because that's how Trophy Girl rolls.

"Evan likes to do his own thing," I say. "That's why he doesn't live with us anymore." It's hard to explain. I bet all Lev sees is Evan's good side, the friendly, funny part of my brother that everyone loves.

I hand him the Sharpie. Lev covers Trophy Girl's hair with black marker and draws a ponytail down her back. I add a dab of pink polish for her hair tie.

"She looks like a man in a pink singlet," Lev says.

I'm about to put a touch of pink on Trophy Girl's lips when the door bangs open.

We both turn. Lev tucks the trophy behind his back as Evan strides into the garage. The argument must have gotten worse, fast. In a second, Dalia bursts out of the house, following Evan to his truck.

"I'm not going to chase after you," Dalia says, but she gets in the truck anyway.

"Don't leave now. You're going to miss the fight," I call. Evan doesn't answer. The garage door ratchets open. The silver truck zooms out of the driveway and speeds away. My mouth is frozen shut.

Lev hands me the trophy. "You got pink stuff on your hand. The polish must be wet. Can you put this somewhere to dry until tomorrow?"

I nod. Tomorrow is the first state qualifier. Our parents

are only letting us stay up for the fight tonight because our age group has a late start at the tournament, one p.m.

I shiver. "I hope I'm not like Evan when I'm a teenager."

Lev nods. He gets it. So I go on.

"Whenever my parents tell him what to do, Evan takes off."

"My mom says teenagers are supposed to do stuff like that. If they fight with their parents, it's easier to leave home after high school," Lev says.

"It's more than that with Evan. He can't stand to lose. Even if it's an argument."

Lev blows on his hands. His breath makes a cloud. "Let's go inside," he says.

I hide Trophy Girl behind some old paint cans before we go in.

"Where were you two?" Mom says, narrowing her eyes. I shake my head because it's not like that. Lev is my best wrestling friend. That's it.

As we wait for the big match, I curl up next to Dad, fighting to stay awake. Lev sits on the floor, leaning against his father's legs.

"Scooch over," Mom says to Cody, squeezing onto the couch.

"Mom, you said UFC's too violent," Cody says.

"I can't miss a historic match. Women are the main event. That's what women's lib is all about."

Coach Billy nods. He's not exactly a feminist, but he does say the boys I beat shouldn't be upset that they lost to a girl. They should be upset that they lost to a better wrestler.

At last, the TV announcer says, "Ladies and gentlemen, this is the main event." Everyone claps. "Touch your gloves. Step back. Good luck to both of you."

When the two female fighters square off, they glare and act like they hate each other. Within seconds, blood is flying. The kicks and punches are fast. I can't keep track. The challenger hits the champ with a punch so hard, I see her jaw shift. Dad, Cody, and some of the others cheer. A roundhouse kick to the ribs and the champ is down. The challenger starts pummeling her head. That's when the ref stops the match.

"It's over?" Cody asks. "It's only round two."

"All that buildup for nothing," Dad says.

Coach Billy complains about how unprepared the champ looked. "The challenger wanted it more. Sometimes drive beats training."

Then Mr. Sofer is saying good night. Lev yawns as he pulls on his coat. "See you tomorrow," he says. His smile has extra mischief in it. Tomorrow, we're bringing Trophy Girl to a wrestling tournament.

CHAPTER 22

Lev

The morning after the UFC fight, Abba shakes me awake. "Time to get up. First qualifier today."

I rub my face hard. I was dreaming.

"Nightmares again?"

"The guy on the bridge was different this time. He had red hair, like Evan." The rest of the dream was like it always is. He stood in the middle of the log bridge, calling me to wrestle.

"There's a story in the Bible," Abba says, sitting on my bed. "Jacob dreams about wrestling all night with a stranger."

"I remember."

I go to Hebrew school in the spring, but during wrestling season, Abba's supposed to teach me so I don't fall behind. Homework comes first, then wrestling, and if we have time after that, we do Hebrew school work.

Abba says, "There aren't many sports mentioned in the Torah. You remember Jacob's dream because it's about wrestling." He stands and stretches. "Your mother says I don't have enough imagination to remember my dreams."

Abba pulls my arm until I'm sitting up. Grover noses the door open, plops onto the floor, and lets out a gigantic yawn.

"Ready to face the day?" Abba says.

"More ready than Grover." I let the dream fade. I have to face real wrestlers today.

In January, there are five qualifying tournaments, all over Maryland. The only way to get into the State Youth Wrestling Championship is to place in the top three for your age and weight at a qualifier.

We drive to an athletic center close to Washington, D.C. When Mickey comes in, she unzips her wrestling bag wide enough for me to see a flash of gold and pink. Mickey touches the pink nail polish with a finger. "I think it's dry."

"Are we really doing this?" It is a qualifier, after all. What if we get in trouble and the refs kick us out?

Mickey's smile is so wide it makes dimples in her cheeks. "Let's do it now, while everyone's busy setting up."

We head to the trophy table, like normal. Mickey gives me the side-eye as we walk.

"Cut it out, Lev," she says in a low voice.

"What?"

"You're acting guilty."

"Am not."

"Then why do you keep looking at Coach Billy?"

"Someone's got to be the lookout."

The table is filled with rows of golden wrestler boys. Mickey leans over as if she's getting a closer look. "Cover me."

"Yes, Evil Mastermind." I point across the table at the largest awards, trying to shield Mickey from view. If anyone's looking, I hope they think we're just really, really interested in the trophies.

As soon as Trophy Girl is in place, we walk away.

"How does she look?" Mickey asks.

I sneak a glance over my shoulder. There she is, tucked into the third row. Pink singlet, pink shoes, black ponytail down her back.

"We earned a pack of Twizzlers."

"Later," Mickey says. "Time for warm-ups." I'm starting to think that Bryan and Mickey would get along well. They're both excellent plotters.

Our team chooses a mat to warm up on. Mickey and I jog around the big circle. Josh and Isaiah run up behind us.

"Oh, Romeo, Romeo," Josh moans. His tongue must be better if he's back to ragging on us.

"News flash," Mickey says. "I'm on *your* team. Romeo and Juliet were from rival families."

"Ooh, she's smart too," Josh says. Instead of getting mad, Mickey takes off after him, chasing Josh across the mat. Next thing I know, she's got him in a cross-face cradle. I can't believe it. They're both laughing. Devin breaks out of the warm-up circle and takes a flying leap onto Mickey's back. Isaiah runs over and jumps on the pile too.

Coach Billy blows his whistle. "Let's go, Gladiators. Focus! Butterfly stretches. Count 'em out."

Mickey drops to the mat and sits next to me for the stretch. Behind us, Josh and Isaiah make kissing noises.

"Zero percent funny, you guys," Mickey says.

I lean closer to her. "We should tell them."

Mickey nods.

When warm-ups are over, I grab Josh and Isaiah. We huddle up, like always, but this time, Mickey's here too.

"Lev and I have to show you something," she says.

"Your engagement ring?" Josh snickers. Mickey punches his arm.

"It *is* gold and shiny," I say, "but it's not a ring."

"Act casual," Mickey says as we walk to the trophy table.

Josh stifles a laugh when he spots the pink singlet. "No way."

"You did it," Isaiah says. "We talked about it, but I can't believe you did it. Way to change the universe." He puts up two hands. He's so tall, Mickey has to jump to slap them.

"You won't say anything when they figure it out?" I ask.

"Course not," Josh says. He hits his chest twice with his fist. "Gladiator Code."

Mickey rolls her eyes at him. "You watch too many movies."

When the matches start, I climb into the bleachers. My notebook's open. All the coaches' voices float up to me. I listen for the words they use when they've got a wrestler on the mat. Tournament after tournament, it's the same, almost like a song.

Whizzer. Cement mixer.
Lateral drop.
Cross-face. Headlock.
Base up, don't stop.
Knees off the mat.
Suck it back.
Break him down.
Wrist control. Get a grip.
Don't reach around.

Lower your level.
Get close, you're too far.
Keep turning. Don't stop now.
Sink the arm bar.
Get the pin. Get the win.
Take shot after shot.
Stay focused. Keep moving,
and don't ever stop.

By the time Abba calls me for my first match, a headache is starting. I lose to a nationally ranked kid named Micah Garvin from Gold Medal Wrestling.

"Do you want to go home?" Abba asks. His forehead is wrinkled with worry.

I shake my head and escape back to the bleachers.

Every wrestler has his losing spot. There are guys, even high schoolers, who hide under the bleachers with a T-shirt draped over their heads like a tent. Some guys cry in the bathroom or find an empty spot in the hallway. They sit with their backs against the wall, knees tucked up, trying to shake off the loss. Others grab their parents' keys, go outside, and sit in the car with the radio blasting.

I open my notebook, tune out the noise of the gym, and make a sketch of myself on the mat, wrestling the man from my dream. This time, he's shapeless, a shadow trying to swallow me up, almost like the vampires I've been studying for Mr. Van's project.

"Hey, Lev."

I look up. Mickey's pulling herself to the top of the bleachers.

"Nice view," she says.

"You say that every time." I'm about to ask how her first match went when Isaiah calls, "Billy the Kid wants to talk to us."

"All of us," Josh adds.

Mickey and I trade a look, something between panic and a smirk. We find Coach at the trophy table, talking with the tournament's organizer. Coach frowns. He's holding Trophy Girl. "You four have been acting up all day. You know anything about this?"

Josh, Isaiah, Mickey, and I stand in a row. No one makes a sound.

The tournament director crosses his arms over his big belly. He stares down at Mickey's bright pink wrestling shoes, then up at the pink nail polish on her fingers. Was she wearing that yesterday? Mickey blushes.

"I'll let you handle this," the director says. He goes back to the head table.

Coach Billy raises an eyebrow at us, his face stern. "It's a warning this time. Don't do it again."

"Yes, sir," we all say. I take the trophy from Coach. He says a few words to Josh in Korean. Josh makes two quick bows with his head.

Coach puts an arm around Mickey's shoulders. "I know it's frustrating, being one of the only girls, but there are better ways to handle it."

"Yes, Coach. Sorry." Mickey nods and her braids bounce. "It won't happen again."

As soon as Coach walks away, the four of us run out to the hallway.

"I'm going to get in trouble for being disrespectful to my uncle," Josh says, "but it was worth it." We all burst out laughing.

I put out a hand. Isaiah puts his on top of mine. Then Josh. Finally, Mickey holds Trophy Girl on top of our stacked hands.

I say, "Fearsome Foursome on three?"

"Is that a thing?" Josh asks.

Isaiah nods. "Oh, it's a thing. Best wrestling prank ever."

"One, two, three, Fearsome Foursome!" we cheer.

Isaiah and Mickey bump fists.

"Where'd you get that?" Nick Spence muscles into our group. All four of us stare at him. His Eagles singlet is like blue ice next to our red Gladiators gear.

"What do you care?" I snap.

But Mickey hands him Trophy Girl. "We made it ourselves."

I wait for Nick's verbal takedown: *That's the only trophy you're gonna take home today, Sofer.* Or *That's supposed to be a girl?* Instead, he examines the trophy, then gives it back to Mickey. "Thanks," he says, and walks away.

"What was that all about?" Josh asks. We burst into laughter again.

Over the next few hours, I wrestle my way back up the bracket, but I end up with fifth place. Mickey's only lost one match. She's still wrestling when Abba says he's taking me home to get some rest before school tomorrow. Before I leave, I tell Mickey, "Trophy Girl needs a friend. Keep winning. Bring a Trophy Boy home so she has someone to hang out with."

"Got it, chief," Mickey says. She gives me a hug. "Feel better, Lev."

As soon as we're away from the noise of the tournament, I do feel better. Before Abba can pull out of the parking lot, I close my eyes and fall asleep.

CHAPTER 23

Mickey

It was a good tournament. For the first time since Kenna quit, I had fun competing. I placed fourth, above Lev, which I may have mentioned to him a few times, or a hundred.

"Brag while you still can," he says.

All week, I think about the Fearsome Foursome and the Trophy Girl prank. At school, when I break into a grin in the middle of algebra, Lalita Parsons is convinced I have a new crush. At lunch, she asks, "Is he from school or from wrestling? Is he tall or short? What color is his hair?"

Kenna rolls her eyes and mouths, *Ignore her.*

Friday is the school talent show. It's also a Gladiators practice night.

"What should I do?" I ask Mom on Thursday. "I'm getting better at every tournament. I can't skip practice now. This could be the one."

Mom stirs our dinner in the slow cooker while she scans newspaper headlines. Cody zips into the kitchen, dunking a piece of cornbread into the pot before Mom can block him.

"This could be the one what?" he asks around a mouthful of crumbs.

"My breakthrough tournament. I got fourth last week. I can make it to States if I push myself at practice. But tomorrow's the talent show. All my friends are going."

"I didn't make it to States till last year, Mickey," Cody says. Mom shoots him an icy look for using my wrestling name in her presence. "Missing one practice isn't going to kill you. Have some fun."

"What do *you* want to do, Mikayla?" Mom enunciates each syllable of my name.

I want to do both.

"Mom, why don't you go sit down?" Cody says. "*Mikayla* and I will set the table." He practically pushes her out of the kitchen. Mom is suspicious, but she takes the newspaper and disappears into the family room.

"Trust me, sis," Cody says, waving Mom's wooden spoon for emphasis. "Cut yourself a break and go to the show. You've gotta have a life outside of wrestling."

I'm still not sure what to do until I see Kenna waiting for me to get off my school bus on Friday morning. She walks beside me into the building. She doesn't say hello, good morning, or how are you. It's all, "You're coming, right?"

"I haven't decided."

Kenna pulls a strand of her curls straight. I haven't seen her do that since the night of the Eagles meeting. "One practice isn't going to make a difference."

I don't answer.

Kenna flutters her eyelashes at me, trying to be funny. "It's your duty as my best friend."

It's too early in the morning for drama, but all the things I've wanted to say to Kenna since wrestling season started come tumbling out of my mouth.

"My duty? What about your duty? You promised we'd be wrestling partners forever. Then you went and quit, and you didn't even tell me. I had to hear it from my mom."

Kenna pulls me toward her locker, out of the flow of sixth graders. "I tried to tell you," she says. "You wouldn't listen. All you cared about was the season starting."

"So it's my fault? We were supposed to move up to travel together."

Kenna unzips her winter coat and fusses in her locker. "I'm allowed to change my mind."

"You still don't get it. Wrestling is really important to me."

Kenna stuffs her coat into her locker and slams the door. She's wearing a black T-shirt with the word *Thriller* hand-drawn in snot-green letters.

"You're the one who doesn't get it," she says. "I wrestled for three years because it's important to you, Mickey. I never wanted to be a wrestler. I just wanted to hang out with my best friend."

That's when Lalita bounces over to us. She's wearing the same T-shirt, advertising their "Thriller" number. "I am freaking out. The show's tonight. Aren't you so glad we did the shirts? They look amazing."

"See you later," I say.

I hurry to homeroom without stopping at my locker, put my head on my desk, and try to breathe. All those years on Coach Brandon's rec team, I thought Kenna loved competing as much as I did. But she doesn't come from a wrestling family. It isn't the glue that keeps the Franklins together, the way it is for us. It's not the only thing she and her dad have in common. To Kenna, wrestling is just an activity. It might as well be robotics club or debate team. But she stuck with it for three years, because of me.

We have each other. Even if we don't wear the singlets. That's what I told Kenna, the night she quit. I have to show her that it's still the truth.

Cody comes to the talent show with me. He struts into the cafeteria and tries to act cool when teachers stop him to say how tall he's gotten. My brother's not the only high schooler who came to the show. When he sees some of his friends, Cody ditches me.

I'm fine sitting with Kenna's parents. We have a great time. There are the usual singers, skits, even a Bollywood-style dance number. Our principal and vice principal sing a duet, "I Got You, Babe." The parents think it's hilarious.

"Thriller" is the last act of the night. In the program, Kenna is listed as Visual Effects Artist. When Lalita and the dancers take the stage, the audience gasps. Kenna's zombie makeup looks spooky, with just the right amount of gore. She must have spent all afternoon doing their faces.

The dancers lie down onstage. Kenna peeks from behind the curtain. When she spots us, she waves to me and her parents. She gives someone a thumbs-up and ducks backstage.

The sound of a creaking door blares through the cafeteria speakers. We hear footsteps, a wolf howling. The zombies stretch. They stumble to stand up, and then they're dancing. The crowd cheers. I've listened to the songs on the playlist Kenna and Lalita made so many times, I know all the words to "Thriller." Mrs. Franklin and I both sing along. I can barely stay in my seat.

When the last evil laugh fades and the show ends, Mrs. Franklin turns to me. "You have a beautiful voice, Mikayla. How did I not know that?"

As we walk out of the cafeteria to wait for Kenna in the hallway, Mrs. Franklin says, "Hearing you sing reminds me of the music videos you and Kenna used to make on my phone. Remember? You'd choose a song, spend hours coming up with a dance routine. I still have the videos somewhere."

"I remember," I say. "It'd be fun to watch those sometime."

Mrs. Franklin hugs me. "You two are lucky to have each other."

When Kenna meets us in the hallway, her dad hands her a bouquet. Her smile is huge.

"Everyone looked amazing!" I say.

"Could you see the makeup okay?"

I nod. I whisper in her ear, "Sorry about this morning."

"Me too," she says. "Talk later?"

Then Lalita runs up to us, her arms open for hugs. She's wearing the pink Prom Scream dress that Kenna and I talked about, all those weeks ago.

"We're having a party at my house, Mikayla," Lalita says. She grabs both my hands. "Please come. Kenna's more fun when you're around."

"I have a tournament tomorrow." I haven't thought about wrestling all night. I wonder who Lev practiced with.

Cody overhears. He raises an eyebrow in my direction. "Go have some fun, Mick."

That's the moment when Lalita realizes this tall guy with red highlights in his hair is my older brother. Her cheeks turn as pink as her dress, even under the gray zombie makeup. I hope Cody doesn't notice. That would be awkward.

We text Mom. As long as I'm home before eleven, she says I can go. When we get to Lalita's house, all the "Thriller" kids are there. Mr. and Mrs. Parsons greet us at the door.

"Whoa," I whisper to Kenna. The Parsons' entranceway is bigger than my whole bedroom. A chandelier hangs high above our heads.

"Wait until you see the basement," she says.

Lalita's parents bring us to the kitchen for pizza—I only have one slice—and soda, which I skip. If I eat junk, I won't wrestle well tomorrow. We head to the basement. There's a huge TV along one wall. Lalita cues up the "Thriller" video and the dancers do their zombie routine for me and Kenna. After that, we gather in a big clump on the couch, some of us cross-legged on the floor.

"Let's play Truth or Dare," Lalita says. She's leaning against Kenna's shins while Kenna braids her dark hair. A shudder goes through my body. I've never watched Kenna braid anyone's hair but mine. She'd better be careful if she doesn't want to get Lalita's gray zombie makeup all over her hands. It's starting to crack and rub off on her pink dress. Gross.

"Who wants to go first?" Lalita asks.

Kenna blurts out, "I'll be right back. Bathroom." She drops Lalita's hair and pulls me off the couch. "Come on, Mikayla."

"Oh. Okay. Start without us," I tell everyone.

As soon as we find the bathroom, I ask, "What's wrong?"

"Truth or Dare. Lalita likes to get in people's business. Asking about crushes."

"That's just how she is." Hasn't Kenna noticed?

"I don't like it." Kenna pulls one of her tight curls straight, then puts the ends in her mouth.

"Are you okay?" I put a hand on Kenna's shoulder. She sits down on the closed toilet lid.

"All Lalita talks about is which boys she likes."

A thought walks into my head and waits for me to find the words I need. "You don't like boys?"

Kenna tilts her head to one side and closes her eyes. "I don't like anyone. I don't think I ever have. At sleepovers, when everyone's whispering about who their crush is, I make it up. Or sometimes I go to the bathroom so I don't have to answer. That's weird, right?"

"We're eleven, Kenna. Everything's weird." She leans her elbows on her knees and puts her head in her hands. I rub her back.

"Lalita makes me feel like I'm not cute enough. Her older sister tells her what clothes to wear and how to put on mascara. I don't have anyone to teach me that stuff."

"Me either. All Evan and Cody teach me is wrestling moves." The thought of Cody helping me pick out an outfit for school makes me laugh.

"I wish we had a coach and a team, someone to show us how to be middle-school girls." Kenna says.

"Is that why you quit wrestling? Because people think it's not a girl thing?"

Kenna looks at the floor. "People look at me. Did you ever notice? They try to figure out what I am. Not who I am, but what. Do I fit in with the black kids or the white kids? I've got enough going on, just trying to feel normal. And now . . . school is different. My body's different." Kenna looks down at her chest, which is hard to miss. "Normal girls don't wrestle."

Kenna has never talked to me about this before. I want to say *I'm normal,* but am I? I don't know any other girls who grew up in a wrestling family like mine. If I had sisters instead of brothers, how would my life be different?

Kenna runs a hand through her curls. "I'm tired."

"Let's text your mom. It's already ten-thirty. No one will care if we leave early."

She nods. By the time we say good-bye, the Franklins are here to pick us up.

Kenna leans her head on my shoulder as we ride home. "You're still my best friend."

"Me too," I say. Makenna and Mikayla forever.

CHAPTER 24

Lev

After two qualifiers, Mickey and I still haven't broken through to the championship round. The highest either of us has gotten so far is fourth place. Not good enough. Isaiah and Devin are both going to States, but Josh is struggling. He had a growth spurt and had to move up a weight class, which stinks this late in the season. As far as I know, Nick Spence hasn't gotten in either. He's still wrestling 90.

Nick is too skinny. I never see him in the school lunch line. He brings a small brown bag to the cafeteria. And he doesn't act like a maniac in PE, the way he used to. I don't think he has the energy. I'm not the only one who's noticed.

"What's Spence doing for his mythology project, the Incredible Shrinking Man?" Bryan whispers to me in language arts.

"That's not funny, Bryan," Marisa says, which makes Bryan blush. Could he be more obvious?

"He does look kind of skeletal," Emma says before Mr. Van hushes our table.

I'm helping Bryan work on the creative writing piece for his Superman project. It's an acrostic poem.

Superhero

Strong man.
Undefeated.
Powerful.
Energetic.
Ready to help.
Hopeful.
Extraordinary force.
Right moves.
On my side.

Maybe Bryan's superhero is his uncle Steven, who loved pro wrestling so much. The person I picture is Evan. I've been asking Dalia to take me to one of Evan's varsity dual meets, so I can watch him wrestle. Finally, she says yes, as long as I promise not to bother her and her friends. That's fine by me. Mickey will be there, so we plan to sit together.

The night of the meet, Dalia's wearing her hair loose. I think she's got makeup or something on her eyes. They're all clumpy. She's puts on Evan's purple Cavaliers Wrestling hoodie. It's so big on her, she looks like a giant grape, but I keep that to myself.

The gym isn't full. It's mostly parents in the stands and some kids in Cavaliers purple. The other team, Glenmont, is in green. There's a girl jogging with their team, wearing

Glenmont Gators sweats. She's got frizzy dark hair pulled into a ponytail. I wonder if Mickey noticed. Everyone's always telling her that hardly any girls wrestle in high school. Maybe that's changing.

I spot Mickey across the gym with Mr. Delgado and the Cavaliers wrestlers. Her dad is the Cavs' team manager. He'll be busy keeping stats during the matches.

Evan's not the biggest guy on the team, but his red hair makes him stand out. He's wearing the T-shirt I got him for Hanukkah. Mickey waves to me, then pulls Evan's arm. He shoots me a smile, points to his *Tell Me What You See When Your Face Hits the Mat* shirt, then sends me a salute. Evan ruffles Mickey's hair before she crosses the gym to sit with me.

When Evan pulls off his T-shirt, I see a huge tattoo across his shoulders.

"Hey, Lev," Mickey says. It's still strange to see her in regular clothes. Mickey's wearing earrings and I think lip gloss. There is no way I'm tying up or grappling with her tonight, even to joke around. What if her earrings get caught?

"What's it say on Evan's back?" I ask.

"*Delgado.* My dad's got a matching tattoo. The lettering they picked has all these sharp edges."

"Ouch."

"I know. Cody wants to get one when he turns sixteen. My dad says it's a brotherhood thing, but my mom hates it." She twists a strand of her hair around her finger. "I'm not going to do it, even if they ask me."

"There's a girl on the Glenmont team," I tell Mickey.

"I know. She reminds me of my best friend. I wish Kenna would come back to wrestling. You'd like her."

"I would?"

"She's the one who usually talks me out of pranks. Unlike some people I know." Mickey grins at me, her red-and-gray braces showing.

The first wrestlers, at 106 pounds, step onto the mat. They're not much bigger than us.

We squeeze onto a bench. Dalia smiles and waves at Mickey with a purple pom-pom. She is never nice to my friends. But I've never been friends with Evan's sister before.

Mickey and I watch every match, talking over the moves we know. Dalia and her friends are the loudest people in the crowd. I can't believe she thought I'd embarrass her. More like she didn't want me to see her screaming her head off and acting like a normal teenager.

The 138 bout is the Glenmont girl versus a sophomore wrestler from Evan's team. It ends in a 3–3 tie. When everyone realizes the match is going into overtime, the bleachers get loud. It's sixty seconds, sudden death. The first person to score wins.

Evan and his teammates cheer, "Pin, pin, pin, pin!" but in the stands, everyone—Gators fans and Clifton High students—is rooting for the girl. She shoots first, gets the takedown and the win. Dalia and her friends shout, "Girl power!"

Mickey points a thumb in Dalia's direction. "Aren't they overdoing it?"

"It was a great match," I say.

"They're making a big deal because a girl beat a boy. It—I don't know—it keeps things unequal somehow. I can't explain." She shakes her head.

"You think too much."

"Someone has to."

The next few matchups are wins for Glenmont. Evan's coach gets more and more upset with each loss. He questions the ref, then complains to Mickey's dad. This is the coach I'll wrestle for when I go to Clifton High. It makes me wish I could stay on the Gladiators forever. Or go back and wrestle for Coach Harvey.

I'd never tell anyone this, but I miss rec league. My team was the Tigers. Twenty-one guys, from Sammy in kindergarten to the eighth grader who was so big we called him Tank. Every week, we had a pin ceremony. When a Tiger won his first match of the season, he'd get a giant pin to put on his wrestling bag. Then, whenever we won another match, Coach Harvey gave us smaller pins to hang from the big one.

Small silver safety pins were for a close match, small gold pins if you won a major decision or a tech fall. There was even a special pin with orange and black beads for coach's discretion. You could earn that one even if you lost, as long as you impressed Coach. But what I wanted, every week, was a big gold pin. We only got those for pinning a kid's shoulders to the mat. All the Tigers clipped the pins on our wrestling bags, where other teams could see. They made a nice, sparkling sound when we walked.

It's not like I can say to Billy the Kid, "Hey, Coach. Why don't we get pins for our wrestling bags?" Gladiators are serious athletes. Still, I miss the fun we had in rec. The Tigers knew Coach Harvey liked us, not only when we won, but because he thought we were good kids. He told us so all the time.

Finally, it's Evan's turn. A couple of wins, and the Cavs could tie up the meet. Mickey grabs my arm and squeezes. Our eyes are glued to the mat. Evan is 170 pounds of solid muscle. He bends down to put on the red ankle cuff and I see the tattoo, *DELGADO* in knife-sharp letters, across his back.

There's a lot of hand-fighting at the start of the match. Evan and the Glenmont guy grab hold of each other's wrists and triceps. Evan keeps reaching for his opponent's head, trying to grasp the back of his neck.

"He's head-hunting," Mickey says.

The Glenmont wrestler's hands move so fast, he accidentally lands a slap on Evan's cheek. Evan steps back and starts to take off his headgear, but Mr. Delgado shouts something at him. I can't hear over Dalia and her friends cheering, "Let's go, Evan!"

The ref gives the Glenmont kid a caution, which means Evan gets a point. They reset. Both wrestlers try a few takedowns, but nobody gets control. At the end of the first period, it's 1–0 for Evan.

"Can you believe they have two-minute periods?" I ask Mickey.

"I know. One minute is long enough."

The ref flips the disk. It lands green side up—Glenmont's

choice. Their wrestler takes down. It's an easier position to score from. Evan needs to be strong. Before the whistle, I see the Cavs coach give him a small, slow nod. Evan nods back before taking the top position.

At first, the Glenmont wrestler keeps his base. Evan chops the right arm, pulling it back to his opponent's waist. Evan's knee drives the kid forward, flattening him out. Next to me, Mickey is clapping, bouncing up and down on the bench.

Now Evan grips the kid's left elbow. The ref stands by their feet, waiting for someone to make a move. He's about to signal a stalemate when Evan spins to the right.

"He's going for the cradle!" I tell Mickey.

"Cross-face cradle. Here it comes."

Evan's right arm hooks forward with the force of a punch. The Glenmont kid recoils. I suck in a breath. The ref blows the whistle and signals blood time. He holds up his left arm again, the one with the green cuff. It's a point against Evan.

Evan's coach runs out to contest the roughness call. My eyes are stuck on the Glenmont boy. Blood drips from his face. Bloody noses happen all the time in wrestling. He'll be back on the mat in a second. But when the Glenmont coach goes to stuff cotton up the kid's nose, he arches back, hands flying to his face.

"Is he okay?" I ask Mickey.

"The ref awarded Glenmont a point, but if he doesn't finish the match, it's an injury default. Evan wins."

"But he's hurt. Evan got him in the face."

Mickey looks at me like I'm nuts. "That's what a cross-face is, Lev."

I shake my head. Evan's arm landed too hard against the boy's nose. Didn't anybody else see it? I look back at Dalia. The pom-poms sit in her lap. When she notices me, there's a pinch between her eyebrows.

The ref calls the wrestlers back to the mat and resets them in referee's position. Evan's still on top, since he had control before blood time. The Glenmont boy's nose is puffed out from the cotton stuffing. His mouth makes a hard line. He must be clenching his teeth. On the whistle, Evan breaks him down again. When the kid's face hits the mat, he shrieks. Then he's flat on his back. Coaches and trainers surround him. The crowd quiets down, but Mickey yells, "Stay focused, Ev!"

The visiting coach talks to the ref, then walks his injured wrestler to a chair. In the center of the mat, the ref holds Evan's hand high. Mickey cheers. But I don't. And neither does my sister.

We leave before the meet's over. When Dalia taps me on the shoulder, I tell Mickey, "I've got to go." I don't wait for her to ask me why.

"You saw that?" Dalia says, as soon as we're in the car.

"We're not supposed to hurt each other."

Dalia rubs her forehead. "The ref missed it. He couldn't see from where he was standing." She starts the car. "Injuries happen in wrestling. When you get older, the guys are bigger. They're strong. Kids get hurt all the time." It's almost like she's talking to herself, figuring something out.

"Not like that," I say. "Not on purpose."

Dalia pulls a pack of tissues out of her purse and hands it to me. "I know you think Evan is this real-life superhero, but he's like a big kid. He's so strong. He doesn't realize."

"He did realize."

Dalia says, "Evan doesn't know his own strength."

"That's what Abba said, that time I knocked you down. Remember?"

When we were little and I hurt Dalia, I was protecting myself. She didn't know how to fight like a wrestler, how to balance her weight and fall safely, but just like when I hurt Josh at practice, I didn't know what I was doing either.

"You're still worried about that?" Dalia gives me a small smile. "Don't be." She reaches between the seats and rubs the top of my head. "We were kids. And you're my only brother."

But I know now, wrestlers are supposed to perfect their moves and wrestle aggressively, but safely. If you throw a guy, it's on you to make sure he lands without getting hurt. That's how Coach Billy trains us. Evan's been wrestling a long time. He knows all this. But he got angry after that Gators kid slapped him. He couldn't let it go.

I wonder if he's like that all the time. Off the mat too. "Has he ever done anything like that to you?" I ask my sister. Dalia is quiet. She knows what I'm asking.

"No," she says. She looks out at the dark parking lot. "I think that's why he likes me. I don't buy that 'I'm a big, tough man' stuff, so he doesn't try it on me."

"For now," I say. "Coach tells us we're supposed to leave it on the mat. After the match is over, no matter how mad you are that you lost, or happy you are that you won, we have to dial down our feelings. Otherwise, how would we go back to normal stuff, like school, and doing chores?"

"What are you nattering on about?"

I shrug. "Feelings. Evan doesn't control his feelings."

Dalia nods at me. "You're right about that." She turns the car on. "Let's go home."

I dream about the bridge. Evan is standing on the log, over the river. He calls me, but I can't hear him over the stormy water. When I move closer, it isn't Evan—with his red hair and friendly smile. It's the shadow-man from my sketch-book, the opponent I drew, like a dark cloud. This time, in the dream, I step onto the bridge until I'm close enough to take a shot, to grab the shadow. But the log is too narrow. If I attack, I'll go down with him. I plant my legs in a strong stance and wait for his move. I know if I fight him, he'll turn me into a shadowy shape without a real face, stuck forever on that bridge.

The next day, I tell Abba I have a headache. "Can I skip practice?" I ask.

He puts down his coffee and studies my face, but I keep my expression blank, like a stiff clay mask. "It's the fourth qualifier on Saturday," he says.

"I know. I'll practice extra hard on Friday."

He nods. "I'll let Coach know."

I power off my phone. Mickey's going to ask where I am, and I don't have a good answer.

CHAPTER 25

Mickey

Lev and his sister left right after Evan's match, but I didn't think much about it. Maybe they had a curfew, or homework.

The Glenmont Gators were fired up after Evan's win. Every match went their way. When Dad drove me home, he told me the kid Evan beat was a Gators captain, and their wrestlers wanted revenge.

I've always been proud that Evan's my big brother. Guys on his team treat him like he's some kind of hero. But tonight, I noticed the way the Glenmont kids looked at Evan after the match. They were angry, and afraid.

It isn't until I get home and text Lev *Cavs lost* that I wonder if something is wrong. He doesn't text back.

I'll talk to him at practice tomorrow, I tell myself.

The next night, Josh, Isaiah, and I are carrying wrestling mats to the gym. Lev's father usually helps the team dads roll out the mats and tape them to the gym floor. But Mr. Sofer doesn't show, and neither does Lev.

"Did Lev say he was going to be late?" I ask Josh and Isaiah.

"We don't talk much outside of wrestling," Josh says. He shrugs. "Maybe he's sick."

"Maybe," I say.

Lev's face was pale when the Glenmont wrestler got hurt. I thought it was because of the blood. Ever since Josh bit his tongue a few weeks ago, even a little bloody nose makes Lev nervous. He chews his headgear strap, or the collar of his T-shirt, which I told him is disgusting.

"Chainsaws! Chainsaws!" Coach Billy calls after warm-ups. He lines us up in weight order, from little Devin to the eighth-grade heavyweights. Once Coach is satisfied with the line, we count off, "One, two. One, two."

"Ones, you're on the bottom. Twos, on top."

With fifty kids in the room, it takes us a while to figure out who's going where. "If I hear talking, you're running laps," Coach yells. "How many guys got a spot at States?" About six hands go up. "That's what I thought. We've got work to do, men. Set up in three rows straight across. Lightest guys, you're in this corner."

Cody warned me about chainsaws. In this drill, I'll end up wrestling every guy in my row, even kids who have ten or more pounds on me.

Milo is my first partner. We set in referee's position, with me on the bottom. There's no music. No talking. The wrestling room is silent. We wait for the whistle. Where's Lev?

Tweet!

We wrestle for one minute. When Coach blows the whistle again, all the top men move to the left and work with a new partner. I stay in my spot and wait for the next top man.

Each guy tries to break me down, but I won't give. Sweaty armpits clamp around my middle. I hold my position. I wish Lev were here. I think about Trophy Girl, sitting in my room, and I smile.

"You think this is funny, Delgado?" Coach says.

"No, sir." I look down at the mat.

Josh is my next partner. We're friendly now, but not enough to talk when Coach is like this. Josh wraps his arm around my waist. His chin digs into my shoulder.

On the whistle, my left hand clamps Josh's wrist against my belly. I put my right hand on the mat, as far as I can reach, then shoot my hips away from him and push Josh to the ground. I know what to do: twist my shoulder to face him, get him in a front headlock. Josh flops like a fish on dry land.

The whistle blows.

Coach shouts. "Way to be, Delgado. Top men, move down!" Josh pats my shoulder and moves to the next guy. I've proved my point. Again. I'm as good as my teammates. If Lev were here, he'd flash me a thumbs-up.

Matches speed by. I keep looking at the door, waiting for Lev. When Coach reverses us and all three rows of bottom wrestlers switch to the top position, I know practice is halfway over. Lev is not coming.

I don't win all my matchups, but I wrestle hard, trying to push Lev's voice out of my head. *Evan got him in the face.*

I try not to see the Gators coach scowling at my brother, like he'd done something wrong. I wrestle hard. I don't care what anyone thinks about my brother, or anything else.

But when practice is over, and we've rolled up and put away the mats, I open my phone and see Lev's message.

Evan broke that kid's nose.

I sit on the floor and type: *Accident. Where are you? You missed chainsaws.*

I saw him, Lev texts.

ACCIDENT.

He doesn't answer. I know Evan acts like a jerk sometimes, but Mom says that's boys being boys. Besides, if Evan hurt that kid on purpose, the ref would have disqualified him.

I'm glad the next day is a school day. It gives my mind a break from wrestling. I try not to think about Evan, Lev, and all the worries swirling in my head.

At lunch I tune out Kenna and Lalita's conversation. Lalita notices I'm not listening. "Are you mad at us?" she asks.

Why does everyone think quiet equals mad? I shake my head and pick at the carrot sticks in my lunch. "Rough practice," I say. "I didn't tell you, Kenna. Last weekend, I almost qualified for States." It feels good to brag a little. To forget that my wrestling partner isn't answering my texts. Or that my brother clocked a kid in the face and maybe broke his nose.

Kenna puts down her yogurt and hugs me.

Lalita says, "That's amazing, Mikayla! This calls for a cookie celebration. I'm buying!" She jingles her Hello Kitty coin purse at me and runs off to the lunch counter.

Kenna tells me all about the beginning hip-hop class Lalita found for us. "As soon as you're done with wrestling, we can start."

Lalita comes back with three chocolate chip cookies. They are gooey and delicious, the one thing our cafeteria is awesome at. All of a sudden, I'm blinking back tears. Kenna hands me a napkin from her lunch bag.

"Lev and I had a fight, I think."

"Oh, no," Lalita says. "The way you talk about him? It's precious."

"It's not like that."

"Uh-huh." Lalita smiles at me.

Kenna slides closer. She gives me a look that means *You can tell me.*

"Later," I say.

It's not Kenna I need to tell, but Mom. If I let her know what happened at the meet, that Lev thinks Evan hurt a kid on purpose to win a match, she's going to flip. I can picture her shouting, *How could you say that about your brother? Delgados are supposed to stick together.*

I call Kenna after school and fill her in. "What am I going to do?" I ask. "Mom and Cody and me, we're finally getting used to living together, without Evan. If I tell Mom what happened, it's going to pull everyone in our family apart."

"You'll do the right thing," Kenna says. "Whatever that is."

CHAPTER 26

Lev

On Thursday, our class meets Mr. Vanderhoff in the media center. We have the whole period to work on our mythology projects. I've been revising my vampire poem, but I haven't shown it to anyone yet.

Bryan and I sit behind a display of graphic novels, where he can stare at Marisa Zamora without her noticing.

I hold my fingers an inch apart. "You're this close to being a creeper."

Bryan smooths back his gelled hair. "I'm doing it today."

"Doing what?"

"Asking Marisa. The social's next Friday." He taps me on the temple. "Hello? Lev? The social? We've been planning this forever."

We have? I shuffle through my memory. I know Bryan's on a mission to talk to Marisa every day, but I forgot about the social. "Sorry. Wrestling brain."

He must be nervous. He's tapping the table with his fingers as if he's playing notes on his clarinet. And last period, he threw out half his lunch.

"Tell me when it's over," Bryan says. I must look confused. "When your season's over, genius. Are you okay?"

I don't tell Bryan I skipped practice last night. I don't tell him about Evan, or Mickey, or my nightmares. It's all stuck in my head. Every time I try to figure it out, the words rush away, like the river in my dream. I change the subject.

"When are you asking her?"

"Now." Bryan stands up. He's dressed up. Instead of track pants and a hoodie, he's wearing dark jeans and an orange polo shirt.

"You look good, man."

Bryan blinks at me and smiles. "I bet you say that to all the girls."

"You're ridiculous."

"That's what you love about me."

As soon as I'm alone at the table, I open my notebook. I added some lines to my poem after Evan hurt that kid. Maybe I should take them out. I'm not sure I want anyone to read this.

Wrestlers are vampires.
Gyms are their caves.
They shut the doors,
stay locked inside,
and don't come out
until day submits to night.
Wrestlers are vampires.
They never see the sun.
They push your face

into the mat until
your nose oozes blood.
They crush you flat,
break you down, bury you.

"How is your project progressing, Mr. Sofer?" Mr. Van sits down next to me. He looks out of place in the media center, like a giant in a chair made of Popsicle sticks.

"I have vampires on the brain."

"A classic monster myth. Man versus his own animal nature." I nod like I understand. He tilts his shaggy head toward my notebook. "May I read what you're working on?"

"Yes. Not out loud, please."

Mr. Van's lips move as he reads. "Interesting," he says. "Dark, but interesting." He points a big finger at my poem. "If I remember correctly, earlier this year, you wrote, *I am a wrestler.*"

"Yeah."

"Here you've switched to third person. *They crush you flat, break you down.* You see? Not *we*, but *they.* You've separated yourself."

"It sounds better that way. I didn't mean anything by it."

Mr. Van's eyes stay on my face too long. When I don't speak, he says, "There's a famous wrestling match in Homer's *Iliad.* Two Greek warriors, Odysseus and Ajax in a test of strength and will, but the match ends in a draw."

"Let me guess. After that, they were best friends."

"They earned each other's respect."

I'm glad when Bryan rushes back to the table.

"Hi, Mr. Van," he says. He's grinning.

"Hello, Mr. Hong." Mr. Van stands up. "Good work, Lev. It's a strong, thoughtful poem." He moves on to the next table of kids.

"Marisa said yes," Bryan says.

"All right!" I put my hand out for a fist bump.

"On one condition." Instead of sitting, Bryan leans back against the table. "We go as a group. You, me, Marisa, and Emma."

"But Emma and I are friends." In elementary school, we were captains of our egg racer team. We were both obsessed with the Warriors books. We planted trees together on a fifth-grade field trip and came home covered in mud. Going on a date with her would be weird.

"As a group," Bryan says again. "Marisa's not allowed to date until high school. It's some archaic family rule." I swear, sometimes Bryan sounds like a page out of Mr. Van's dictionary.

"So she's telling her parents we're going as a group?"

"Exactly."

"When's the social again?"

"Next week. Friday night."

In the front of my wrestling notebook I wrote the dates of the state qualifiers. There are only three more chances. This Saturday, and next Saturday and Sunday. Bryan reads the dates and frowns.

"I can't," I say. "Unless I qualify this weekend, I can't go. I'll need to practice that night. It could be my last chance."

"You've been practicing all season. It's one night." Bryan

crosses his arms over his polo shirt. "It's important, Lev. I wouldn't ask you if it wasn't important."

"I know. Sorry," I say. I am sorry, but wrestling comes first. Bryan knows that.

"Forget it." Bryan gathers his binder and notebook.

"Where are you going?"

He doesn't answer. He weaves through the bookshelves, looking for a spot at someone else's table.

I stare at the dates in my notebook.

<del>Sunday, January 8</del>
<del>Saturday, January 14</del>
Saturday, January 21
Saturday, January 28
Sunday, January 29
MARYLAND STATE CHAMPIONSHIPS, February 11–12.

I wish I could tell Bryan that ever since Dalia took me to Evan's dual meet, stepping on the mat is the last thing I want to do. But Bryan will say, *So, quit.*

It's not that simple. It would be safer to go to the social, play badminton, and goof around. But that's not going to earn me a chance to be a state champion. Once you're a state champ, no one can take that away from you. It's part of who you are, for the rest of your life.

Bryan doesn't meet me at my locker before lunch. All around me, kids are laughing, yelling, talking. Usually I can block it out, but today, the noise is like fingers grabbing the sides of my head. There's a sharp jab in my shoulder. When I turn, I see Nick Spence.

"I'm going to crush you this weekend, Sofer."

I try to blink away my headache, but it won't go. "You're moving back to 95?"

Nick flops his hair from one side to the other. "It's a better weight for me." I can guess what that means. He hasn't been able to qualify for States at 90 pounds.

"Okay." I move to walk around him, but Nick blocks me.

I see Bryan pass by on his way to lunch. "Bryan!" I yell, but he swerves into the crowd.

"I need to talk to you about your partner," Nick says.

"Talk to her yourself. You'll see her on the mat on Saturday."

Nick grips my arm. My hand shoots out and catches him behind the neck. I didn't mean to do that. I've wrestled Nick so many times. It's a reflex.

Before either of us can move, a hand lands on my shoulder. Mr. Van eases the two of us apart. "On your way, Mr. Spence. You'll be late for lunch." He turns Nick around and sends him down the hallway.

"Still nursing a rivalry, I see," Mr. Van says.

"Yeah."

"'An enemy who gets in, risks the danger of becoming a friend.'" Mr. Van's voice is deep and comfortable. I know he's trying to calm me down, but quoting poetry at me won't help.

"That's not going to happen, Mr. Van."

"Give it time." He strokes his beard, then walks away.

I slam my locker shut. Mr. Van doesn't know what he's talking about. Why didn't Bryan come over to help me deal with Spence? He's supposed to have my back. I know he's mad about the social, but that doesn't mean Bryan and I are done being friends, does it?

CHAPTER 27

Mickey

Lev is the first person I look for at practice. He and Isaiah are carrying a mat to the gym. Devin rides the rolled-up mat like a cowboy, waving one arm in the air. I laugh and head over to help them. Then I sit with Isaiah, Josh, and Lev, lacing up my pink wrestling shoes.

"It hurts my eyes every time you put those on," Josh says.

"You should talk. Yours are neon yellow. It's like someone took a highlighter to your feet."

Isaiah cracks up, but Lev is silent. I slap him on the back and say "Let's go" when Coach calls for drills.

"I'm working with Milo tonight," he says.

Josh gives Lev a sideways look, then turns his back on him and faces me. "C'mon, Mickey. You and me."

The two of us find an empty spot on the mat. I'm trying to be a good partner for Josh, but I keep wondering why Lev is upset with me. Evan didn't do anything wrong.

I find Lev in the hall during water break. He's holding Devin up to the fountain.

"Stop avoiding me," I say, when Devin finishes drinking

and runs back to the gym. "We're on the same team, Lev. Same weight class."

Lev fills his water bottle from the fountain. When he's done, he says, "Spence is wrestling 95 tomorrow."

"So?" Is that what he's upset about?

"Just telling you." He starts to walk away.

I follow. "What's wrong? I thought we were friends."

"Nothing's wrong. I'm tired. That's all." He stops and rubs his shoulder. "I run out of steam this late in the season, right around qualifiers."

"That's only part of it," I say. "You've been ignoring me, like at the beginning of the season. But this time, it's 'cause you're upset with Evan."

Lev shakes his head.

"Yes, you are. You think you're better than everyone, Lev Sofer."

Lev takes a step back. "What? No. I don't. My record stinks this season."

"I'm not talking about wrestling. You think you're better in here." I poke him in the chest, hard. "You judge people. Nick. And now Evan."

Lev pulls away from me.

"I'm just telling it like it is."

He turns around and goes back to the gym.

I'm alone in the hall, gulping air. Finally, I have a wrestling friend and I go and blow it. I let my mouth control my brain. I've got to get Lev to talk to me. But as soon as practice is over, Lev and Mr. Sofer are out the door.

"Why's Lev being such a butt-wad?" Josh asks while we roll up mats. "Did you two break up or something?"

"I have no clue," I lie.

I'm quiet in the car on the way home. Mom puts on our favorite Broadway cast recording, *Bye Bye Birdie*. She tries to get me to sing along with her, but I close my eyes and pretend to sleep.

"Want to talk about it?" she asks when we get home.

"Can I shower first? I feel gross." The truth is, I need a few extra minutes to figure out what I should say to Mom. How am I going to explain what's happening with Lev, when I don't understand it myself? He's so full up with anger about Evan that it's spilling over onto me.

"I'll make us hot chocolate," Mom says.

I take my time in the shower. Am I going to tell Mom what happened at the dual meet? What if she yells at me for snitching on Evan? I don't know if I can handle that. What makes it worse is that Dad was at the match. If I tell Mom what happened and she agrees with Lev, that Evan injured another wrestler on purpose, she'll be furious with Dad. He should have stopped Evan somehow. If I open my mouth about the match, my parents might get in a big fight.

Kenna says I'll do the right thing, but I don't know what that is. Wrestlers are supposed to be strong, and fearless, but I'm eleven. This is way bigger than I am.

By the time I'm in pajamas, I've decided. I'm going to tell Mom what I saw and that's it. What Lev thinks is his own business. But when I come downstairs, she's standing in the kitchen in her pink bathrobe, arms wrapped around Evan. He's not supposed to be here tonight. His red head is bright against Mom's shoulder. Is he crying? I stop in the doorway.

"Dalia broke up with him." Mom pats his back.

"Mom, I need to talk to you. You promised." It's not fair. Evan left to go live with Dad. He can't show up and take Mom whenever he feels like it.

Mom hands Evan tissues. He wipes his eyes and gives me a sad smile. "Hey, Mighty Mite. I'm a mess."

Part of me wants to run over and wrap my arms around his middle, the way I always do. The other part wants to scream, *What about me? I'm a mess. I need Mom too.*

Cody walks into the house. He's about to throw his wrestling bag on the floor when he freezes and stares at all of us. He puts up his hands and backs down the hall. "Whoa. I'll come back later."

"Give me a few minutes with Evan," Mom says to me.

I pound up the stairs. Cody is right behind me.

"Why does he do that?" I ask my brother.

"Do what?"

"Take over. Evan has to be the best. He's a better wrestler than us. He's cooler than us. Mom loves him more than us."

Cody follows me to my room. He's grown so much, he fills up the doorway. "Okay. I'm Next Man Up. Talk to me." Cody pushes his sweaty hair out of his face.

"Fine." I sit cross-legged on the floor.

Cody sits too, his knees up against mine. "Mickey, Mom doesn't love Evan more than us. She just misses him."

"She lets him get away with stuff. Everyone lets him get away with stuff."

"How do you think I feel? I'm stuck being the middle kid between Number One Son and the Little Princess."

I throw my plushie hedgehog at him. "I am not a little princess."

"I know. You're Mighty Mite. I think you're tougher than any of us."

"Really?"

"Really." He tosses Spike the hedgehog back to me. "You can tell me, you know. I'll listen."

"You're not going to like it."

"Try me." Cody leans against my bed. His sweaty, disgusting St. Matt's Wrestling shirt is touching my bedspread, but I let it slide. I tell him everything that happened at Evan's dual meet, what I saw, and what Lev thinks. I tell him how Lev skipped a practice and wouldn't partner with me tonight.

"Lev thinks Evan hurt that Glenmont wrestler on purpose. And now he's mad at me, because I'm sticking up for my brother."

Cody whistles. "And Dalia goes and breaks up with him. That is way too much drama." He pulls my bare feet into his lap and pinches my big toe. "What do you think? Did Evan hurt that kid?"

I fill my chest with air and blow it out. "Maybe." I look at Cody. "Should I tell Mom? Dad was there. He saw what happened and didn't say anything. It could get ugly."

Cody tilts his head to his shoulder. "Mom might not

even believe you. She doesn't always think straight when it comes to Number One Son."

I nod, relieved. Cody understands.

"I could tell her for you."

"Thanks," I say. Cody's trying to protect me. It makes me feel better, knowing he would do that. "I think I have to tell her myself."

He swings his arms and pops up to standing in one motion. "You've got this, sis. You're a tough kid."

I hold up my hedgehog. "Spike says you're a good brother, Cody."

CHAPTER 28

Lev

What I told Mickey, that I'm running out of steam, is true. I could never say it to Josh or Isaiah. They'd think I was weak, or start quoting Billy the Kid at me. "Give it all you've got." It's the Gladiators' motto. I don't know if I've got enough strength to finish this season.

Mickey's the only person who might understand, but instead of listening, she yelled at me, said I think I'm better than everyone.

For a long time, I convinced myself it was everyone else's fault that I didn't make States last year. I blamed Nick for taunting me at tournaments, teasing me at school because I cried after a hard loss. I blamed Coach Billy for telling me to take a shot when I wanted to turtle up and stall. But now I see that was my fault too. Last year, at the end of my first travel season, I had no fight left when it came time to beat Spence.

I trudge up our front steps after practice. When Abba opens our front door, the smell of chicken soup rushes out to greet me. Mom has a rule. She doesn't cook after eight p.m., but there she is, in the kitchen, wearing her cup-cake apron. There are carrots and a carton of eggs on the counter. A big soup pot sits on the stove.

"It smells good," I say.

"*You* smell like teenage boy," she complains.

I catch Abba shaking his head and frowning at Mom. He's telling her, *Bad day. Don't tease Lev.* They do this all the time, talk to each other without words. Will I ever know someone well enough to do that?

Abba looks in the pot. "Saaba's matzo ball soup?" He grabs a chunk of carrot off the counter and lobs it into Grover's waiting mouth.

I'm confused. "We only eat matzo ball soup at Passover."

"Dalia needs comfort food," Mom says. She slides an elastic off her wrist and pulls her hair back. "She broke up with Evan. It's too late for candles, but we are going to sit down and have Shabbat dinner, even if it's ten o'clock at night."

"Why'd she do that?" I ask, but I think I know the answer.

"Shower first," Mom says. "Then we'll eat, and we'll talk."

Abba dips a spoon into the pot and takes a sip. He kisses Mom's cheek. "I'll check on Dalia," he says. He pushes me up the stairs. "Go shower. The steam will be good for your headache."

He's right. The rushing water drowns out the ringing in my ears, chasing away the noise of practice, the rubber smell of wrestling mats. But it can't change the fact that I was mean to Mickey, that I'm not any closer to making States and proving I'm better than Nick Spence.

You think you're better than everyone, Lev Sofer.

Dalia and Abba are still upstairs when I get back to the kitchen, dressed in my pajama pants and T-shirt.

"I'm glad she broke up with him," I tell Mom.

She turns her Future Guidance Counselor eyes on me. Maybe Mom thinks if she looks at me long enough, she'll get X-ray vision and see inside my head. "Why would you say that, Lev?"

I lean down and press my face against Grover's soft ears. "Evan's not safe."

"Come sit."

I follow Mom to the table and rest my head on my arms like a pillow.

"Dalia told me about the meet," Mom says. When I don't say anything, she lifts my chin up. "It's not going away, honey. You can't sleep it off, or wrestle it away."

My stomach is tight. "Mickey says it was an accident. But that's not true. I saw him do it, Mom. The ref missed it."

She takes my hand and wraps it in her palms. "That's okay. It's what Mickey needs to believe," she explains. "Evan is her brother. As much as it hurts you to see that Evan isn't perfect, think how your friend must feel."

I hold my breath for a second.

"Give her time to deal with it her own way." Mom stands up and smooths her apron. "Ready for soup?"

I nod. Maybe this counseling stuff Mom is learning isn't all bad. She might actually be good at it.

Dalia and Abba come to the kitchen. We sit at the table long after blessings, long after our soup bowls are empty, and Dalia explains what happened with Evan. It wasn't the dual meet. That was only the last thing. On the night of the party, Dalia saw the way Evan argued with his father, then stormed out of the house.

"He would've left me there, if I hadn't followed him," she says. "And then he wouldn't go back and work things out. We drove around half the night. It took him hours to calm down. I don't have time for that."

I lean against Mom.

"Bed for you," she says.

"Not yet."

Dalia says, "This is what I want." She spreads out her hands and waves them over the table. "I want to sit at the table and talk. We can be mad at each other and eat soup and work things out."

Abba laughs. "That's why they say chicken soup is good for the soul."

This is what I want too. More family dinners on Shabbat. Fewer Saturdays stuck in a gym, pushing myself to break some kid down until he's flat on the mat. But I can't break up with wrestling the way Dalia can with Evan. I've been part of the sport since I was seven years old. It's who I am.

CHAPTER 29

Mickey

Mom comes to my room first thing on Saturday. She sits behind me on the bed, braiding my hair for the tournament.

"I'm sorry about last night, Mikayla. We never had a chance to talk."

"I noticed."

Mom's coffee breath is comforting and familiar. If I don't say anything, we can stay like this. Me, Cody, and Mom get along fine. So what if Evan comes home every couple weeks and sweeps us all up in his problems?

Mom begins to hum. It's "Edelweiss," a song from *The Sound of Music*. She used to sing it to me when I was small. And that's when I know, no matter what I say, Mom loves me.

I turn to face her. "I have to tell you something. It's about Evan. You're not going to like it."

Mom's face tightens. She rolls her shoulders. "I'm ready."

When I lay out the whole story for her, all she does is nod.

"Why didn't you tell me sooner, Mikayla?"

Spike the hedgehog sits in my lap. I squeeze him in my hands. "I was afraid. You say I have to be loyal to our family no matter what. And you and Dad always put Evan first."

Mom starts to protest, but I stop her.

"Okay. Not always, but you do. When he messes up like this, gets so angry or upset that he doesn't think straight, you make excuses. It's not good for him. And you push me and Cody out, but we know what's happening."

Mom looks in her lap, instead of at me, so I put my hand over hers.

"Is Evan going to be okay?"

"He's going back to Dad's today."

"Oh."

"It's not perfect," Mom says. "But Evan needs Dad. Your father may be obsessed with sports, but underneath he's a gentle man." She closes her eyes. "I'm glad you told me, honey. You're right. We have to make some changes. I'll talk to your father. Speaking of which"—Mom stands up, full of energy again—"he'll be here in thirty minutes."

"Dad's taking me to the qualifier?"

"He insisted. He said this is The One."

I hope Dad is right. If I place in the top three today, I'll be the youngest Delgado ever to make States. Maybe, now that I told Mom what's been bothering me, I'll be able to focus and wrestle.

Dad and I are quiet in the car. I asked Mom not to speak with him until we get back. It's an hour-long drive to Frederick. I listen to the playlist of songs Kenna and Lalita made for me at the beginning of the season. Dad drinks his coffee. We get there with plenty of time to weigh in. I've been creeping up on 95 pounds this month. Dad raises his eyebrows at me. I have to make sure I stay under 95 for a couple more weeks. I don't want to be like Josh Kim, struggling in a higher weight class right at the end of the season.

I climb to the top of the bleachers, but Lev's not there. The buzz of the tournament feels far away, like I'm standing on a tall building. All the people and their noise are far below, where they can't touch me.

So this is why Lev likes it up here, I tell myself.

When Dad comes to get me for my first match, he waves a hand in front of my face. "Find your focus, Mickey. Whatever's bothering you, put it aside."

"I'm fine, Dad. I'm ready." I've been holding so many things inside. I can't wait to get on the mat and take it all out on someone.

My first bout is close. I lose by one point.

"You should've had that," Dad says. I pull off my headgear and hair cap, but before I can shake my braids out, Dad puts his hands on either side of my head. "You're wrestling sloppy."

I've seen him get in Evan's face, and Cody's, at tournaments, but he's never done it to me. Dad's nose is close to mine. I see his red-brown stubble and the tight muscles in his neck. My eyes prickle. I can't cry at a tournament.

"You didn't wrestle to win. You've got to convince yourself you can win, no matter who's across the mat from you. Doesn't matter if it's a boy, a girl, or a hedgehog." He puts a hand on my forehead and smirks. "You got me?"

I blink the tears away. "Yes, Dad."

"You'll have to wrestle yourself out of a hole if you want third place."

Dad sits in his canvas chair and types notes about my match into his phone. Dad's paying attention, real attention, for the first time. He can be harsh, but I know he wants to help me get better.

I come up behind the chair and put my arms around his neck. "When's my next match?"

Dad hands me the phone. I look over the bracket again. I see Lev's name, and Nick's.

"I'm going to find Lev."

When I'm sure Dad's busy with his phone, I duck out to the concession stand, buy a pack of Twizzlers, then climb up the bleachers.

This time, he's there, sitting in his usual spot.

"Nice view," I say. Lev doesn't answer. "I wasn't sure you were coming until I saw the bracket sheet."

I hold out the Twizzlers. Lev pulls a couple of red twists from the pack. We lean against the wall, staring at the crowd while we chew.

"My father was the one who got Evan into wrestling," I tell him. "He wrestled too, when he was in high school. It was the one thing he and Evan kept doing together, after Dad moved out."

I nibble the end of my Twizzler. I can't tell if Lev's paying attention, but I keep going. "Then Cody started. All the custody time Dad was supposed to spend with us on weekends?

It was at wrestling tournaments. I used to have a Wonder Woman backpack for tournament days. It had coloring books, Go Fish cards, and a sleeping bag. Evan would make a bed for me across the bleachers and half the time I fell asleep."

"Why did you start wrestling?" Lev asks.

"I wanted to be like my brothers. Being a Delgado means being a wrestler. What about you?"

"I used to get occupational therapy, when I was little," Lev says, without looking at me. "I couldn't handle loud noises, or lumpy foods like mashed potatoes and bananas. But I liked crashing into stuff. I was always banging into kids on the playground. The OT told my mom I should try wrestling."

We're quiet for a minute. "Evan's not a bad person," I say. My eyes are prickling again.

"I know." Lev grabs another Twizzler from the pack. "It still wasn't right, what he did."

"I know," I say, "but it's complicated. When you're on the mat, when your head is trapped between some kid's sweaty arm and his ribs, it's hard to think about right and wrong. I just want to get out. I want to get out and beat him, no matter what it takes."

"I don't know if I'm like that," Lev says. "If that's what it takes to win, maybe I'm not a wrestler, after all."

"You are a wrestler, Lev. I've learned so much from being your partner." I stand up. "I have a match soon. Want to warm up with me?" But Lev is already leaning over his notebook.

I win the next match. When I check the updated bracket sheet, I see that Nick lost to the same kid who beat me this morning. That means he's my next opponent.

I jog back and forth along the mat, where Josh Kim is wrestling a kid from the Gold Medal team. The ref raises Josh's hand. I step up to the judges' table. A mom with long black hair and a Gold Medal Wrestling shirt blinks her big mascaraed lashes at me.

"Aren't you precious with your pink wrestling shoes and knee socks? What's your name, sweetie?"

I refuse to smile at her. "Delgado."

Isaiah's mother takes the timekeeper's seat next to Lash Lady. Lev runs up to the table carrying a duct-taped towel. He nods at me. He must be helping to keep time. His dad is busy volunteering on another mat.

In our corner, Coach Billy picks me up by the shoulders, the way Dad always does when he's coaching me or my brothers. He squeezes me, stretching out my shoulders until my feet leave the floor.

Nick Spence checks in at the judges' table. He looks to the Eagles' corner. Dr. Spence has his arms crossed over his chest. I'm surprised to see Nick's sister there too. She tugs on her father's sleeve and says, "That's the girl with the pink shoes." I smile and give her a wave.

I hear Nick tell the judges, "I forfeit."

Isaiah's mom stops setting the clock. "Forfeit on what grounds?" she asks.

"There's no rule that he has to give a reason," Dr. Spence barks in his tight voice. "I would know if there was."

All the adults crowd around the table: Coach Billy, Dr. Spence, and the ref. I see my father making his way over there too, but Coach Billy waves him off.

I wish someone would tell me what's going on. Are they going to make Nick wrestle? I need to stay warm, so I take a few shots and try to block out all the voices. But I hear Coach Billy tell Nick, "You're in the consolation bracket already. If you forfeit, you're out."

"Don't speak to my son," Dr. Spence says. "He does not have to wrestle a female if he doesn't want to."

While they argue, Nick runs over to his sister. He pops off his headgear and puts it on her head. The way she smiles at him reminds me of me and Evan, when I was little.

I try to catch Coach Billy's attention. I want to tell him Nick can forfeit if he wants, as long as I get a win and move up in the bracket. But Lev finds me first.

"Don't let 'em mess with you," he says. His cheeks are flushed. He takes my arm and walks me over to Coach. Lev stands tall, with his shoulders back. He taps Coach Billy on the shoulder.

"Spence hasn't wrestled Mickey all season," Lev says. "He forfeited matches and cut weight so he wouldn't have to wrestle her."

"Lev, stay out of it," Coach says.

Lev ignores him and turns to the ref. "Why should he be allowed to forfeit? So what if she's a girl?"

The ref shakes his head. "I can't stop him from forfeiting a match, son."

Dr. Spence stares at me, arms folded. In the stands, I hear people grumbling. Dad is talking to some of the Eagles parents he knows. They're pointing at the mat. Some people are booing. I can't tell who's on my side and who's with the Spences. I spot Josh and Isaiah talking nearby. I wish I could join them, but I can't walk off the mat until the ref calls the match.

"Coach, say something," Lev begs Coach Billy. "Do something. You can't let them treat a Gladiator this way. Mickey works harder than anyone."

I know Lev hates Nick Spence. I know he's upset about Evan. He wants to do the right thing, but even the grown-ups don't know what the right thing is. He should save his anger for the mat, but he won't stop running his mouth.

"Tell the wrestling board to change the rules! Stand up to the Spences!" Lev shouts at Coach. "Why are you afraid of them?"

The voices in the stands are getting louder.

"I need to talk to my wrestler," Coach Billy tells the ref. He pulls Lev off the mat and out of the gym.

There's a small smile on Coach Spence's face. Next to him, Nick's sister covers her ears with both hands.

"Are we wrestling?" the ref says. He's tapping his foot on the mat.

Nick shakes his head.

The ref meets me in the center of the mat and holds up my hand. I pop open my headgear, pull on my Gladiators hoodie and shorts. I want to talk to Josh and Isaiah, but instead, I end up chasing after my father. He stomps out of the gym, ranting about outdated rules. "I need some air. I'm going to the car to cool off," he says.

That afternoon, I wrestle like a beast. I work my way up to third place in my weight class. My trophy may not have a girl on top, but I did it. I made it to the state wrestling tournament.

I can't wait to tell Lev, but he texts me first.

I quit Gladiators.

I shiver and pull my jacket up over my head like a tent, so I can see his words glowing on the screen. I grip my phone tight and type. *Why?*

He doesn't answer.

Thanks for sticking up for me, I write. There's no reply.

CHAPTER 30

Lev

This is the first time all season Abba and I have driven home in daylight. There's a field in the distance full of giant windmills. They're taller than trees, moving with the wind. Watching the blades spin helps my thoughts settle.

Coach reamed me out in the hallway this afternoon. He said I was disrespectful and made him look bad in front of the other coaches. He said if I was upset about Spence forfeiting, I should have talked to him privately. Instead, I caused all this "drama."

Where has he been all season? The drama didn't start with me.

I can still feel Coach's hand clamped on my shoulder. "I'm angry now," he said, "but we'll work it out."

"I don't want to work it out. I don't want to wrestle anymore."

Coach Billy's eyes were dark but not mean. "No, Lev. Number one, you're a Gladiator. Number two, you can't help Mickey if you quit." He held me by both shoulders, so

I couldn't look away. "Middle school is the hardest age for wrestlers. You're going to tournaments, competing against studs from states where wrestling's practically a religion."

He didn't understand. Wrestling wasn't fun today. Every time I stepped on the mat, I saw the guy from Glenmont High, his face covered in blood.

"Promise me you'll hold out for high school," Coach said. "You'll be wrestling guys who are new to the sport, and you'll be the stud."

Coach didn't look like Billy the Kid anymore. I saw frown lines on his face, a knot of muscle on his forehead.

"I don't want to lose you, Lev. You're a good kid, a good wrestler. You know that, right?"

But I don't know it. Not anymore. My stupid plan to mess with Nick Spence, to beat him by helping Mickey, it backfired. Nick keeps finding ways to avoid wrestling her, and now she hates me. I was so mean to her this week. I acted like what happened with Evan was Mickey's fault.

You think you're better than everyone, Lev Sofer.

Abba keeps checking on me in the rearview mirror.

"Stop looking at me," I say. I can't wait until I'm old enough to sit in the front of the car. Thirteen. It's a big year. I get to move up to the front seat, and I'll be a bar mitzvah.

I wrap myself in the blanket Abba keeps in the backseat, fold my pillow behind my head, and dig out my notebook. I don't feel like a vampire wrestler anymore. I don't feel like anything.

I start a new poem.

Who am I
if I'm not
a Gladiator?

Who am I
without
this sport?

I don't
even know.
It's so

much
of who
I am.

I don't
have anything
else.

Abba sends me to the shower when we get home. From the serious look he gives Mom, I know he's going to tell her what happened. They ask me if I want to go out for dinner, as if it's a special occasion.

"Let's stay home," I say.

I play with Grover as Mom and Abba make a salad. Dalia is at an indoor field hockey clinic. This is how it's going to be two years from now, when she's in college. Me, Mom, Abba, and Grover.

"How about a walk after dinner?" Abba asks. He points at Grover. "Just the guys."

It's one of those strange warm nights we get sometimes in the middle of winter. All I need is a hoodie, no coat. Grover woofs at the door while Abba clips on his leash.

"What happened today?" Abba asks.

"I don't know. It felt like everything was crashing down on me." The moon is big above the trees. I remember the owl I heard, that morning at the start of the season. Abba said it meant I would wrestle smart. He was wrong, for once.

Grover stops to sniff a tree and Abba waits in the light of a streetlamp. I stay in the tree's shadow and stick my hand in the light, making shapes on the ground.

"What do you love about wrestling?" Abba asks.

I shrug. "We don't talk about that, even me and Josh and Isaiah. We brag about winning, but never about what it feels like when a kid's pinned under you, kicking like he can't breathe. We never talk about how hard it is to lose." I walk along the edge of the shadow, one foot in front of the other, with my arms wide.

"You'll be twelve this summer," Abba is saying. "When you're thirteen, you become a man. That's our tradition."

"Abba, you know the other night, when we sat at the table and ate soup and talked? I wish we weren't so busy with sports. I wish we had more time like that, the four of us together."

Abba nods. "Competition makes your sister happy. Your mother and I assumed the same was true for you. But you're not your sister."

Don't my parents know how different Dalia and I are? Abba says when something is bothering me, he sees it on the mat. I can't focus. Dalia is the opposite. It doesn't matter if she has a fight with my mom or a big test, when it's game time, all she thinks about is winning.

Abba pulls me close. "Mom and I value you much more as a person than as an athlete."

"You're not mad that I quit?"

"You stood up for your friend. I'm proud of you," he says. "Whatever you decide about wrestling, Mom and I support you. We just want to make sure you're thinking it through. Do you really want to quit? Or are you acting out of anger?"

This is Abba's superpower. It's not extreme strength, or speed, like the superheroes Bryan's doing his mythology project on. Abba gets me to talk about difficult things, because he wants me to think about what's right and what's wrong.

"I'm still having that nightmare," I tell him.

"Some people say it wasn't an angel Jacob was wrestling, but himself."

"Abba, what does that even mean?"

He grins and turns for home. "Do I look like a dream interpreter to you?"

"No. You look like Abba."

"Good."

When we pass the Hongs' house, I ask if Grover and I can go visit Bryan. I ring the bell. Grover sniffs at empty flowerpots. A red-and-gold braid is looped over the door handle. It must be time for Chinese New Year.

Bryan opens the door. "Hi."

Even though it's January, he's wearing shorts. His T-shirt is sweaty. The Hongs have one of those movable basketball stands. For someone who's not interested in playing on a team, Bryan's out here a lot. He leans down to pat Grover's head. "Hi, fuzzbutt," he says. Grover's long tongue shoots out and covers Bryan's hand with a lick. "Ugh. Slobbery."

"Grover misses you."

"It's wrestling season. We're both used to it."

I kick the concrete step, to make myself say the words. "I quit Gladiators."

"Why would you do that?" Bryan pushes his glasses up his nose. He grabs his basketball and comes outside. I tie Grover's leash to the doorknob. He's happy to lie down and take a rest after our walk.

Bryan and I take turns doing layups. "So what happened?"

"Too much drama. Also, I may have mouthed off to my coach."

"That's not good." Bryan passes the ball to me. "Does this mean you're free Friday night?"

"It means I'm free every night."

"School social?"

"Yeah. Gotta have something to look forward to." No more Gladiators. No more States. No more Josh, Isaiah, or Mickey.

By the time Bryan and I are done talking, we've got solid plans for the social.

It's the strangest week of my life. When I'm at school, or if Bryan's free, everything is great. Bryan, Emma, Marisa, and I get permission to eat lunch in the media center so we can work on our mythology projects. It's still warm enough to play basketball or ride bikes after school. But after dinner, I don't have anything to do. I get my homework done and delete texts from Mickey. I don't know what to say to her, so I say nothing. I watch the History Channel, then go to bed early.

I don't even want to open my wrestling notebook, because then I'll have to ask myself who I am. The kid who writes poetry, who thinks it's not worth it to fight? Or the athlete, working to show everyone that I'm the best because—win or lose—I tried my hardest. I'm still not sure. What I do know is I'm a better friend since I stopped wrestling, at least to Bryan and Emma.

CHAPTER 31

Mickey

I get to practice early on Monday night.

"Hey, Mickey." Coach puts out a hand for me to slap. "State tournament! Way to be." He squats down so we're eye to eye. "I owe you an apology."

"You do?"

He scrubs at his goatee. "I don't tolerate disrespect from my wrestlers, but I thought about what Lev said. I should have dealt with the Spences a long time ago."

I nod and rock back on my heels. Finally!

"I sent an email to the head of the county wrestling board," Coach says. "We'll start there, see what we can do." He stands up and puts a hand flat on the top of my head. "The sport's changing, Mickey. More girls want to give wrestling a try."

"Yes, Coach."

"So—how about the Girls' Folkstyle Championship? It's Saturday. Want to wrestle?"

I've heard about Maryland's all-girls tournament, but I figured Coach wouldn't go if I was the only Gladiator there.

"Really?" I can't help it. I jump up and down like a kangaroo.

"I'll talk to your parents," Coach says. "The last state qualifier is Sunday, but you're already in. You can wrestle Saturday, bring home a trophy—one with a girl, I bet—and take a rest day on Sunday. How's that sound?"

"Awesome, Coach!"

"What was that all about?" Josh asks when we're putting on our shoes.

Since we're friends now, I don't mind teasing him. "There's a special tournament on Saturday. Invitation only, and Coach picked me to go."

Isaiah gives me a fist bump, but Josh glares across the gym at his uncle. "How is that fair? He didn't ask me."

I let Josh's face scrunch up in a frown before I hit him with the news. "That's because it's the state girls' championship."

"Is that a real thing?" Josh says. I shove him and he falls into Isaiah on purpose.

"You heard from Lev?" Isaiah asks, pushing Josh off him.

"He's not answering my texts."

"My mom took me to see him yesterday," Isaiah says. "I've never been to his house before. He's got this fat old beagle. Cute dog."

"You saw Lev?" Josh asks. "My uncle was pretty upset. Did you hear the way Lev talked to him at the qualifier?"

"He didn't mean to be rude," I say. "He was standing up for me. No one else was willing to do that." I turn to Isaiah. "Is he coming back?"

"My mom talked to his mom while I was there. His parents think he needs a break, is all. Maybe he'll be back next week."

"But what did Lev say?"

Isaiah looks down at his shoes. "He's beat. Not just tired-beat, but up here." He looks at me and touches his forehead. "You know how Coach always talks about killer instinct? It's like Lev got the killer instinct knocked out of him."

"But he'll miss the last qualifier," I say. "He needs to practice."

"He'd better come back," Josh says to me. "Otherwise I'm stuck with you for a partner."

I go to shove him again, but Josh rolls out of my reach. Then he's on his feet, hands up, ready to wrestle. I'm up too. We grapple until Coach blows the whistle to start practice.

I watch the door, but Lev doesn't come.

CHAPTER 32

Lev

Bryan and I decide to go classy for the social. The day after I quit, we talk our moms into taking us shopping for bow ties. Real ones, not clip-ons. Bryan's tie is black with musical notes. Mine is navy with paw prints. We watch a YouTube tutorial and practice tying each other's ties.

After dinner that night, Mrs. Oliver and Isaiah stop by. I introduce Isaiah to Grover, and then we play video games in the basement while the parents drink tea and talk. He wants to know if I'm quitting for real, but I don't have an answer.

"You know how Coach is," Isaiah says. "The second he's done yelling, he forgets what he was mad about."

"It's not about Coach. Wrestling's not fun anymore, at least not at tournaments. I still like hanging out at practice with you and Josh and Mickey."

"Fearsome Foursome," Isaiah says, holding out his hand for a fist bump. "It's not going to be the same without you. We need you to keep Josh in line."

"Mickey can handle Josh."

"It's not the same."

On Friday, we turn in our mythology projects. Mr. Van knows how stressed out our class has been. We play musical chairs for the rest of the period. Instead of music, Mr. Van recites Edgar Allan Poe's "The Raven." When his voice pauses, everyone dashes to get their butt in a chair.

Marisa is meeting us at the social, because it's not a date, but Bryan and Emma come to my house to get ready. All our parents want to take pictures. Emma loves the bow tie idea so much, she's wearing one too. It's pink with black mustaches. Mrs. Hong and Mom gush about how cute the three of us look dressed up, even if we are wearing jeans and high-tops with our button-down shirts and ties. With the three of us back together, it almost feels like middle school never happened.

When we get to Meadowbrook, Marisa is in the art room. The tables are set up for card games: Uno, Pokémon, and Magic: The Gathering. Bryan pulls at my sleeve and whispers, "The girl of my dreams is playing Pokémon. I am on a non-date with Marisa Zamora and we are going to play Pokémon."

I give him the side-eye. "This must be what nerd heaven looks like. See you later. We're going to the gym."

Emma and I challenge a couple of her chorus friends to a game of badminton. We ask Mr. Wilebsky to be the referee. "It's good to see a smile on your face, Sofer," he says.

I try to ignore Spence playing half-court basketball on

217

the other side of the gym. He's staring at me, but since I quit wrestling, I don't care what Spence does.

Marisa and Bryan rush into the gym, practically tackling me and Emma. "The karaoke contest is starting," Marisa says.

I let Emma drag me to the door. "Marisa and I have been practicing our song for weeks," she says. "Come cheer us on."

I rub my arm. Emma's got a strong grip, probably from running around with a lacrosse stick all the time. I should have asked her to join the Gladiators. Then Mickey would've had another girl on the team.

In the cafeteria, Mr. Van is in charge of karaoke. Bryan and I crack up when we see him. His badger face doesn't go with his Hawaiian shirt and plastic lei.

While Emma and Marisa sign up for karaoke, Bryan gets us lemonade and cookies. I stand to the side of the cafeteria, away from the bright stage lights.

Nick Spence finds me. "I need to talk to you." He pushes his floppy bangs out of his eyes.

"Fine. Talk."

"I want to go to a Gladiators practice."

I almost snort. "Why? You hate us." *Not us. Them,* I tell myself. I'm not a Gladiator anymore.

Nick shoves his hands in his pockets. "My little sister wants to wrestle," he says. "She wants to join a team and my dad won't let her." He looks right at me. "You know how he is."

I nod. "You want to see how Coach and the guys treat Mickey."

"Yeah." He flops his hair.

"Won't your dad find out?"

"I'll tell my father I'm going to your house for a school project."

There are a million things I want to say: *Won't your dad notice when you come home sweaty from practice? Doesn't he know we hate each other?*

"I saw how you stood up for your partner," Nick says. "I can do that for my sister. I need to. She looks up to me."

"I can't invite you to practice, Spence. I quit the team."

His eyes pop wide. "What'd you do that for?"

"When I back-talked my coach last weekend, he lost it. I just . . . I couldn't take it."

Nick kicks a loafer against the concrete wall. "I *want* to wrestle Delgado, you know. Anna, that's my sister, I want her to see that it's okay. But my dad's old-school. My mom's not around and he thinks being a single parent means he's got to be a total control freak. He hates change."

Archaic, Bryan would say.

"Sorry, man." I put a hand on Nick's shoulder. It's the first time I've touched him without trying to knock him to the ground.

"Maybe I could talk to her," Nick says.

"You mean my *girlfriend*?" I crack a smile. Nick smiles back.

"She's a good wrestler."

This was supposed to be my night off from thinking

about Coach, and Mickey, and whether I made a mistake. I could call Mickey, tell her about Nick's sister, but I can't stop thinking about what she said to me.

You think you're better than everyone, Lev Sofer.

I'm not better than Nick and he's not better than me. We're both trying to figure stuff out.

"I haven't talked to Mickey much since I quit."

"But you'll help me?"

"I'll think about it."

I wish the social didn't have to end. Everything I've missed out on since I joined the Gladiators is crammed into three hours. Friends grabbing my arm, dragging me over to play cards and badminton, asking me to listen to them sing. I'm outside, waiting for my parents to pick me up, when Mr. Van comes lumbering out of the building. "Nice shirt, Mr. Van!" I call.

"Mr. Sofer. Did my eyes deceive me or were you having a parley with Mr. Spence?"

"I don't know what that is, but I talked to him, yeah."

"Remember Joy Harjo's words. 'An enemy who gets in, risks the danger of becoming a friend.'"

"We're not exactly enemies anymore."

"You've let go of your black-and-white thinking. Smart."

Mom's car pulls up.

"Have a good night, Mr. Van. And thanks."

Mr. Van is wrong. There is a lot of black-and-white thinking happening in my brain. It's telling me that quitting wrestling means cutting off my Gladiators friends, including Mickey.

When I get home, I make myself text her. It's been more than a week since we fought and I'm not sure she wants to hear from me. The only thing I can think of to say is sorry.

CHAPTER 33

Mickey

Mom says I can invite Kenna and Mrs. Franklin to the girls' tournament. I should have invited Lev too. He finally wrote back to me. It was only one word, but maybe if I'd invited him, he would have said yes.

I've never been to an all-female tournament before. The gym is filled with girls. They're braiding each other's hair in the stands, drilling together on the mat. I see girls with compression shirts under their singlets, some with pink boots like mine, and more than one *Wrestle Like a Girl* T-shirt.

When Coach Billy walks in, Mom sighs. "He's so cute."

"Ew. Mom, that's my coach." I do not like the grin on her face. "Lev and Isaiah call him Billy the Kid."

Mom tilts her shoulder to her cheek. "Still cute," she says. "Don't worry. He's too young for me."

Coach spots us. When he shakes Mom's hand, I glare at her. She'd better not embarrass me. She gives me a wink.

"Ready to get out there and crush these girls, Mickey?" Coach asks.

When he says "crush," I stifle a giggle. I bet he has no idea my mom has a crush on him.

I take out my headgear and shoes. Next to us on the bleachers, a group of refs is reviewing the rule book. There are at least eight of them: old, young, black, white, an Asian guy, but not one woman.

"Girls are more flexible," one of them says. "You'll see 'em twist out of a pinning combination that'd end the match for a boy."

I spot a girl sitting alone on top of the bleachers. She looks friendly enough. I'm going to go for it.

"Nice view," I say when I get up there.

She smiles and closes her book, *Harry Potter and the Order of the Phoenix*. It's my favorite in the series. I like her already. Now that I'm up here, the girl looks a little older than me. She's Indian, maybe. Her skin is more olive than Kenna's. Her hair hangs down her back in a thick, dark braid.

"My partner and I like to sit up here too," I tell her.

"Where is she?" the girl asks.

"He. I'm the only girl on my team."

"There are two of us on my team," she says, "but the other girl is my sister, and she's only seven." She points out a little girl in a purple singlet. "I drill with a boy too."

"I'm Mikayla." It feels strange, saying my full name. When I'm wrestling, I tell people I'm Mickey. But with no boys around, I can be my real self. Dad's not here, so I don't have anything to prove. Today, I get to wrestle because that's what I love to do.

The girl smiles again. "I'm Supriya. We drove down from Connecticut last night."

"Connecticut? Isn't that like five hours away?"

"Six! My dad said we couldn't pass this up. He's my wrestling coach. He coached my brother too, but he's in high school now. My father didn't want to give up the team, so my sister and I joined."

"Want to warm up?"

Supriya and I jump off the bleachers. We jog around the mats together, then find our bracket sheets. There are only five girls in my age and weight class.

Supriya waves good-bye to get ready for her first match as Kenna and her mom walk in. They have a surprise for me. Lalita is here too.

I give them all a gigantic hug. "I'm so glad you're here."

Kenna's in jeans and her Mustangs Wrestling T-shirt from rec league. Seeing our old team logo makes me smile.

It's clear Lalita has never been to a wrestling tournament before. Even though it's almost February, she's going to be way too hot in that fluffy blue sweater and thick black leggings. Her eyes are bugging out. "There are so many people here," she says. "I thought you were like the only girl wrestler in the state."

Kenna and I laugh. I introduce my friends to Coach Billy. Lalita sits with the moms, but Kenna comes with me and Coach as we scout out the wrestlers in my bracket.

"I hear you used to wrestle, Kenna," Coach says. "We could use a few more girls on the Gladiators. Mickey's got her hands full."

Kenna says, "I've heard about the stinky, sweaty boys." That makes Coach laugh.

"I told you he's nice," I whisper, as we follow Coach Billy across the gym and watch one of the matches.

"This girl right here, she's winning, but she's a defensive wrestler," Coach tells us. "She waits for her opponent to make a move, then—BAM!—scoops up the leg when the other girl is off-balance." Coach looks at me. "How do you handle a defensive wrestler?"

"First shot, best shot."

Coach knows what he's talking about. In my first bout, I come out strong against the defensive wrestler and catch her by surprise.

The ref is lying on the mat next to us. I push her shoulders down and look up at him. Is he going to give me the pin? The buzzer sounds. The ref holds up three fingers and touches them to his back, awarding me three points. I'll take the W. My bracket's so small that one win puts me in the championship round.

"That was amazing!" Lalita says after the match.

"You've gotten so fast," Kenna says. "I could never wrestle with you now."

My next opponent is from a Pennsylvania team. Coach Billy says, "They're well trained. She's going to be tough. Push yourself and keep fighting."

I step onto the mat and put on the green cuff, glad to have my lucky color. Maybe it's a sign that this is my moment.

The Pennsylvania wrestler gets me with an ankle pick

in the first few seconds. I manage to move out of bounds. The ref sweeps his arms to the side, whistles, and calls us to reset in the middle. He holds up his red cuff with three fingers raised. It's not even the end of the first period, and I'm down 5–0.

"Keep it together," Coach calls out. "No quitting."

Delgados aren't quitters, I tell myself.

The ref flips his coin. Red is face up. My opponent chooses down position. I try everything—chopping her arm, sinking a half—but she breaks my hold and gets the escape. Another point for her.

I take neutral stance and tell myself not to panic. If I can't overpower this girl, maybe I can outsmart her. I fake a shot to the leg. She moves to block me, and I spin her to the ground, shoulders first.

"Takedown. Two!" the ref shouts.

She's on her back and I'm on top. She's not a defensive wrestler. Instead of bridging her stomach to the ceiling to knock me off, she panics and kicks wildly. It's too late. The ref hits the mat. The bout is over.

"Woo-hoo!" Coach yells, pumping a fist in the air. "You know why you won? Undefeated spirit. You didn't let the points get in your head."

My cheering squad—Mom, Mrs. Franklin, Kenna, and Lalita—are jumping up and down in the stands. I think the moms might be crying.

Supriya from Connecticut finds me when the awards are handed out. We take a picture of both of us holding first-place trophies. I want to go celebrate with Kenna and Lalita, introduce them to the Delgado donut tradition, but Mom can't wait to get out the door. There's a snowstorm coming and she's nervous about the weather. Before we go, Coach Billy pulls me aside one more time.

"Would you to talk to Lev for me, Mickey?" I almost correct him and say my name is Mikayla. "I've spoken to the Sofers a few times, but so far, he hasn't changed his mind."

"He won't talk to me either, Coach."

"Try again. We can't give up on him."

Holding on to my giant, not-nail-polished, first-place Trophy Girl, I tell Coach, "Okay."

I'll figure out a way to bring Lev back to the Gladiators.

At home, Evan is waiting at the kitchen table. I've got my trophy in one hand and a box of donuts in the other.

"How's it going, Mighty Mite?" he asks. "Or should I say Girls' State Champ?"

"You should say Girls' State Champ."

I hold out my trophy.

"Cody!" Mom shouts up the stairs. "Little help with the groceries? Evan, you too."

"Donut first?" Cody calls.

"Donut after. Earn your keep," Mom says.

I pour three glasses of milk while Mom, Cody, and Evan unpack the bags. Then Evan comes to sit with me. We munch on our donuts.

"Mom and I talked," he says. "We're still buddies, right?"

"You're my brother." I tap my finger on his hairy arm. "Can you do me a favor?"

"Name it."

"I know Lev's sister broke your heart and all."

Evan closes his eyes. "I don't like where this is going."

"Can you talk to him? Lev, I mean." I'm not sure what to say. I need to stop worrying about hurting my brother's feelings, and think about my friend. "He got shaken up. Ever since your dual meet."

Evan nods. "So I've heard."

"He quit the Gladiators."

He doesn't say anything right away. "I didn't know that." Evan finishes his milk and wipes his mouth with the back of his hand, like a little kid. "What do you want me to do?"

"Tell him not to give up."

"Hit him with the old 'Delgados aren't quitters' pep talk?"

I put my head on my brother's shoulder. "How about the old 'I made a mistake, please forgive me'?"

"It's like that?"

"Yeah. It's like that. He won't talk to me, Ev. But he might listen to you."

"I'm the fallen hero."

"Not if you get back up and fix it."

CHAPTER 34

Lev

"Coach Billy sent me another email this morning," Abba says on Saturday. My parents are watching the Weather Channel. They've upgraded tonight's snow prediction to a blizzard. "Tomorrow's the last qualifier. You're sure you don't want to go if this storm is a bust?"

"Yes."

"Have you talked to Mickey?" Mom asks.

"I texted her."

My parents give each other a look. Sometimes I think they're not happy unless they're worrying about me.

I hate to admit it, but my first nonwrestling Saturday has been dull. I can only play video games for so long before I itch to get up and move. Mickey hasn't texted me back yet. Is she at a tournament? Did she make States?

By dinnertime, it's starting to snow. Dalia and I set the table. No weigh-ins for me tomorrow. For once, I eat as much spaghetti as I want, two big bowls full, covered in meat sauce.

"Can I go to Bryan's?" I ask after we eat.

Mom's wearing sweatpants. Her hair is in a messy

ponytail. Now that she's between semesters, Mom's more like her old self. I'm glad she has a few weeks off. She earned it.

"Have you looked outside, Lev? It's coming down sideways."

"It's not like I'm going to get lost walking across the street," I argue. But after a rumble of thunder, I know I'm stuck inside tonight.

When I wake up the next morning, snow is pressing against my window like it wants to come inside. Everyone else is asleep, but Grover needs to go out. I grab a shovel, put on my hat, coat, and gloves, and head into the storm. Ice pellets hit my face. It's so quiet. I feel like I'm the only person in the world.

When I let Grover out, snow gathers on his eyelashes. He runs down the path I shoveled, ears flapping. The second he's done with his business, Grover heads inside. Abba is waiting for me with a mug of hot chocolate.

"How much is out there, do you think?" he asks.

"It's up to my knees and it's still snowing."

"There's supposed to be more snow tonight."

The blizzard lasts all day. I text Bryan. He complains that his mom is making him practice clarinet. I complain that my mom wants me to do a jigsaw puzzle with her, but I don't really mind. I can only spend so much of the day wondering if quitting Gladiators was a good idea. Especially when Mickey sends me a one-word message: *Partners.*

By Monday morning, the storm is over. The snowplows are out, but we don't have school.

I let Grover outside and breathe in the cold air. The snow is like a sheet of paper where nothing has been written. Today, I can decide what I want to do and who I want to be. Am I still a wrestler? And if I'm not, what's my thing? Everyone has a thing. Bryan has music, and his crush on Marisa. Emma has lacrosse. Mr. Van has his poetry and that club he wants me to join. I've spent so much time wrestling, I don't know what else I'm good at.

When Grover's done, I run upstairs to get my notebook. Dalia is sitting on my bed in her panda bathrobe.

"Don't quit," she says. "You're just having a bad season."

"Worse than bad." I sit next to her.

"You love wrestling. You've kept every trophy. Your first pair of wrestling shoes is hanging on the back of your door."

"It's too late. The last qualifier was yesterday."

She rolls her eyes. "Don't be an idiot, Lev. There's two feet of snow on the ground. There was no qualifier."

"So?"

"So Evan says they're rescheduling. He thinks you should wrestle."

"You talked to Evan?"

She twists her braid around a finger. "We're not going out, but that doesn't mean we're not friends." Dalia hands me her phone. "Here. He sent you an email."

"You're letting me use your phone."

"Just read it. I trust you." Dalia tousles my hair and leaves me alone to read Evan's message.

Hi, Lev.

Mickey told me you quit Gladiators. If you
want to quit, fine, but don't do it because
you lost control and can't figure out how
to fix it. When they reschedule the last
qualifier, I hope you get yourself there.
You told me you wanted to make it to States.
You stood up for my sister. Now be a man, and
stand up for yourself.

Your pal,
Evan

I read the email five times. At first, I'm mad. Why
should I listen to him? Then I remember what Mr. Van
said. *You've let go of your black-and-white thinking.* Evan is
trying to fix things. I let his words sink in. It's time to
stand up for myself, leave it all on the mat, and see what
happens.

I put on track pants and running shoes. Dalia and
Mom are sitting at the kitchen table with a bunch of college brochures. Dalia raises an eyebrow at me. I give her
back her phone.

"I'm going for a run." I pull a knit cap over my headphones.

"The sidewalks aren't clear. It's too slippery to run,"
Mom says.

"I'll be careful."

It's bright out. Snow covers the neighborhood. Grover stands in the doorway and whines.

"Not this time," I tell him. I punch up AC/DC on my phone and set off into the cold.

I run through slush, around icy patches, past the basketball hoop at the end of Bryan's driveway. The freezing wind makes my ears ache, but there's blood pumping through my muscles.

Abba said one way to look at the story of Jacob's dream is that he's wrestling with himself. I've been wrestling with myself too. Out here, running with nothing to look at but blank snow, I know I can get back on the mat. And when I do, I'll know what's right for me.

When I get home, Abba tells me the last qualifier has been moved to next Saturday. I have no team, no coach, and five days to get ready.

Mickey's stuck at home too. We set up a video chat.

"Coach Billy wants you back," she says. "You needed a break. It's okay. Everyone understands."

"That's not going to work. I need to focus. I can't do that around Josh and Isaiah."

"But who's going to coach you? Your dad?"

"I was thinking maybe Evan."

I see Mickey smiling on my screen. She nods. "I like that idea. He's at my dad's today. There's a practice mat in the basement. It's perfect."

That afternoon, the roads are clear enough that Abba can drive me to Evan's house.

There's no school on Tuesday, or Wednesday. Plows are still clearing some of the roads. Every day, I meet Evan right after breakfast and stay at his house until dinner. There's no Gladiators practice, so Mickey trains with me.

Evan has a clipboard with a plan for each training session. We drill in the basement for hours, take breaks to eat and play a few video games, and then we're back downstairs.

On Wednesday, Mickey brings her girls' Folkstyle championship trophy to show me.

"Do you think I have a chance at States?" she asks.

I pretend to scrub my goatee like Coach Billy. "You win right here in the practice room, Delgado." She punches my arm, but not too hard.

Evan shows me how to get out of defensive mode, how to attack my opponent with control. "It's something I'm working on too," he says. We haven't talked about the Glenmont dual meet. But when Mickey and I work on cross-face, Evan says, "You're hesitating, Lev."

I sit back and let Mickey up. "I don't want to hurt her."

Evan kneels down. "Take top," he says. I rest my chest against his broad back.

Evan takes my right arm and pulls it across his forehead. "You're aiming up here. If you're just slamming your arm around, you could hurt her, but you're not going to do that. You know why?"

I shake my head.

"Because you're a thinker, always planning your next move."

Mickey nudges Evan's butt with her wrestling shoe. "Tell Lev."

Evan and I both sit up. "I emailed that kid," he says. "The one from Glenmont. I didn't mean to hurt him. I lost control."

Mickey nudges him again. "Evan offered to pay his doctor bills."

"You did?"

"I'll have to get a summer job. It was a clean break, no surgery, but yeah."

Evan says he'll lend me an old singlet for the qualifier, since I can't wear the Gladiators one. "What if it doesn't fit?" I ask.

"You can borrow my Wonder Woman singlet," Mickey says.

I chase her around the mat until Evan claps his hands and sets us up for the next drill.

On Saturday, I wake up to the sound of rain. There's mist from the evaporating snow. For the first time this season, Dalia is coming to a tournament. Evan's meeting us at the Naval Academy's athletic dome. All the kids who still hope to earn a spot at States are here.

I weigh in, put my headphones on, and warm up to AC/DC. Evan's job is to watch the match numbers and manage my bracket. My job is to stay focused.

Across the dome, I see Spence running stairs on an

empty set of bleachers. He comes over while I'm putting on my headgear.

"Did you think about what I asked you, Sofer?"

"Yeah. I haven't figured anything out yet, but I'm working on it."

"I'm going to crush you today." He grins. "No hard feelings."

I put out my hand. "May the best wrestler win." Nick grips my hand and we shake.

No matter how I feel about wrestling tomorrow, today it's good to be back. I'm wrestling well. I win my first match by a major decision.

As I warm up for my bout against Nick, Coach Billy comes over. He's here with a few Gladiators who still hope to earn a spot at States. With his beat-up ears and big shoulders, he looks like an actual gladiator.

I'm not mad at Coach anymore. It's not his fault I lost to Nick last year. He was right, I was wrestling defensively, waiting for the other guy to make the first move. If I hadn't taken a shot, the ref would have called me for stalling and given Nick a point.

Coach puts an arm around my shoulder. "You'll always have a place on my team, Lev," he says. "Once a Gladiator, always a Gladiator."

"Thanks, Coach."

"Go get him." Billy the Kid slaps my shoulder.

I put on the red ankle cuff. Spence is across from me. He puts the green cuff on, then bounces up and down, slapping his thighs. We set in neutral.

The whistle blows. Nick puts a palm on my forehead and I grab the back of his neck, pushing my elbow into his chest.

In my mind, I hear Coach Billy's voice. *Don't let him get in your head.* I understand what that means now. Think for myself. Wrestle by my own code.

Nick tries to grapple with me, but I pop his elbow up and duck underneath his arm. I hold tight to his head, spinning him to the ground.

"Two!" the ref shouts.

I keep his head locked up and drive my knee into his butt. Nick's face hits the mat. He points to his nose. The ref stops us, signaling blood time.

My gut drops. I look at Evan.

"It's okay," he says. "Stay cool."

Dr. Spence is plugging Nick's nose in the other corner.

I can't help it, I'm cautious for the rest of first period and into second. Nick gets a reversal on me, tying the score, 2–2.

I hear Abba and Dalia shouting my name from the stands, but Evan's voice is the one I focus on. "Control," he says. "Be aggressive, with control."

I've got one minute to do this. From down position, I move on the whistle, stepping a foot up until I'm standing. Nick's hands are clasped in the middle of my stomach. I dig my thumbs into his grip, pushing his hands apart.

"Break that!" Evan shouts.

I feel Nick's hands slipping. He tries to hold on, but I'm out.

237

"One!"

It's a point for me. I turn to face Nick, but the buzzer sounds. It's over. We meet in the middle of the mat and shake hands.

"Good match," Nick says. I pat him on the back. Then the ref is raising my hand.

I did it. There's no big celebration. Evan shakes my hand. Abba nods at me. I can tell he's proud.

My next match is a close one against a girl from Navy's youth team. We go two rounds without a score. At the start of the third period, I'm down man. I sit out and get one point for the escape. I can grapple and stall for the rest of the period, or use what Evan taught me and go on the attack.

I take a shot on her leg, pull it against my chest. She reaches for my ankle, but I'm too fast. I trip her standing foot. She's falling. For a second, I hesitate, make sure she lands safely.

"Short time!" Evan calls. "Get your two."

I catch the girl around the neck as she goes down, pulling her into a cradle. My arm hits the mat, cushioning her head. She's more flexible than a boy, but because I trained with Mickey, I know what I have to do to get the takedown.

When the match clock buzzes, the ref is holding up two fingers. I look at the judges' table: 2–0.

People in the stands are cheering, but not for me. "Great match, Jules!" the Navy parents yell.

I shake hands with her. "You've got fans."

She smiles. "They think girl wrestlers are tough, even when we lose."

I shake hands with her coach, then jump into a hug from Evan. He lifts me off the ground.

"You did it! You're in! State championships, here we come!"

"I've got one more match, Evan."

He picks me up again and shakes me. "States! States! States!"

Dalia is jumping up and down. "You two make a great team," she says to me and Evan. As my sister hugs me, I remember what Dalia told me. Evan is always trying to measure up to the wrestler he was in eighth grade. I get that now. *This is my best moment,* I tell myself.

"Do the Gladiators parents cheer for Mickey like that?" Dalia asks me.

"Yeah, but they're not that loud." Maybe they should be. An idea is forming in my head. I find my pen and write a few lines in my notebook, so I don't forget.

Evan sits next to me.

"You're a good coach," I tell him.

"You're easy to work with."

"You should coach wrestling. For real."

He pushes back his red hair. "I do need to earn money this summer. Maybe I'll help out at a wrestling camp. But first, we've got to get you and Mickey ready for States."

"Will you be mad if I don't go?"

Evan's head snaps back in surprise. "Why wouldn't you go? You earned it."

I don't know how to explain it. I pushed myself harder than ever this week. But now I've done it. I earned my spot at States, beat Nick Spence. I came back and showed myself I could wrestle hard and win. If I go to States, it's going to be more of the same.

"I just—I don't want to wrestle." As I hear myself say the words, all the tightness in my chest relaxes. I gave it another chance and figured out I'm done. I don't want to wrestle. Not next week. Maybe not ever.

Evan nods. He's always taken me seriously. "Okay," he says.

There's one more person I have to tell. Bryan.

I used to think it would be the coolest thing, competing at States with Bryan there to see what a great wrestler I am.

On the school bus, I tell him I'm skipping the big tournament. "I know we had a deal," I say. "Don't be too disappointed."

"No worries," Bryan says. "But if you ever go pro, I want ringside tickets. Free ones."

"Hey, can I ask you something?"

"You want me to manage your pro wrestling career?"

"I'm serious, Bry. When I wrestle with you at the bus stop, and in front of school, is that okay?"

Bryan shrugs. "Not really. When we were little it was kind of fun."

"You didn't say anything."

"You never asked me before."

"From now on, if I have the urge to tackle you and push your face in the dirt, I'll ask first. Deal?"

Bryan smiles. "Deal."

CHAPTER 35

Mickey

The night before States, I sleep over at Dad's house. Ever since I qualified for the tournament, he's been coming to Gladiators practice once a week, helping Coach Billy get our team ready for States. Early tomorrow morning, Kenna's coming over to braid my hair. Then Dad will drive us to the tournament.

Evan's out tonight, so Dad and I sit alone at the kitchen island, eating bowls of cereal for dinner. Dad's place is okay. The furniture's fine, but everything is brown and navy blue. The walls, the carpets, even the shower curtain. His idea of decorating is putting his jujitsu bag in the corner. When I'm here, I miss Mom's colorful couch pillows and the vase of flowers she keeps by the front door. It's cozier at home.

Dad puts his elbow on the counter, inviting me to arm-wrestle. I grab his hand with both of mine and force his arm down with all my 95 pounds.

He whistles. "Look out! Mickey Delgado is gonna storm the state championships."

"You've got that right," I say. "But, Dad, can you call me Mikayla?"

"No more Mickey?"

"It's babyish. And I'm tired of having two names."

Dad clears away our bowls and spoons. "Your mother will be thrilled."

"She's coming tomorrow, right?"

"Everyone's coming. Mom and Cody. Evan's going to pick up Lev. You'll have your own fan club."

I take a deep breath. If I was brave enough to talk to Mom about Evan, I can be brave enough to remind Dad of our deal.

"Dad? I know you're Evan's team manager right now, but can it be my turn next season?"

"What do you mean?"

All I want is for Dad to treat me the same as my brothers, to be a member of the Delgado Fearsome Foursome. "You said if I showed you I was serious, that I could compete with travel kids, you'd help coach my team. You'd be great. You know way more than the other dads who volunteer. And you promised."

Dad kisses the top of my head. He hasn't done that in a long time. It was like a switch flipped in his brain when I finished elementary school. I wasn't his little girl anymore. I don't think I'm anyone's little girl, but it's nice that I don't have to feel like a big kid all the time.

"You're right. It's your turn," Dad says. "Evan's got to figure things out on his own. I'll talk to Billy. Also, I have a surprise for you."

I sit up tall at the counter, trying to peek as Dad pulls a red gift bag out of a cupboard.

"Open it." Dad's trying not to grin.

The bag is light. I reach past the tissue paper and pull out a white T-shirt. On the shoulders, *DELGADO* is printed in knife-sharp letters.

"Are you crying?" I ask my father.

"What if I am?"

"I love it." I get off the stool and give my father a gigantic hug.

In the morning, Mrs. Franklin drops Kenna off. Dad makes Kenna hot chocolate while she does my hair.

"I'm super proud of you," Kenna says. "No matter how you do today."

I close my eyes and feel the familiar pull and tug of her hands on my hair. It's like things used to be, the two of us getting ready before a tournament. When it's time to leave, we sit in the back seat of the car, sharing my headphones so we can both listen to the tournament-day songs she and Lalita chose for me.

The state championships last for two days. My age group wrestles today. Little guys like Devin get their turn tomorrow. With nearly a thousand kids in this tournament, it's not easy finding Lev. It still doesn't feel right that he's not wrestling. He earned the right to be here. Lev is my friend, but that doesn't mean I understand him.

Kenna and I walk the loop around the top of Towson University's basketball arena, taking it all in—the bright lights, the yellow seats. Music blares over the sound system. Eight mats cover the basketball court from end to end.

"This place is huge," she says. "I'm glad you're the one wrestling and not me. Look at all these people."

Lev runs up to us. "Whoa! Cool shirt," he says. "It looks just like Evan's tattoo."

"Kenna, this is Lev," I say. Yeah, it's awkward. We're middle schoolers. The way Kenna's looking at him, trying to figure out if Lev matches all my descriptions. Brown hair, freckles, funny ears. He's wearing jeans and a grass-green polo shirt. It looks good on him, but I realize I was hoping he'd change his mind, that I'd walk into the arena today and Lev would be wearing his Gladiators singlet and red shorts, that we'd be warming up together with the rest of the team.

I'm relieved when Lev starts talking.

"I've never wrestled in a stadium like this," he says. "It's the big time. You must be pumped."

"I am. And freaking out. This place is enormous. Did you see the upper level?" I turn to Kenna. "The top of the bleachers is the best place to sit at a tournament. Lev taught me that."

"Let's go check it out," he says. The three of us run up to the highest row of seats in the arena.

"Nice view," Kenna says.

Lev and I can't stop laughing. Finally, we explain our inside joke to Kenna.

"Lev always says that."

"*You* always say that."

"Where's your notebook?" I tell Kenna, "Lev is a poet." I can tell she's impressed.

"I didn't think I'd need it today," he says.

We sit for a minute, but Lev seems antsy. "Let's go back down. This is too far from the action. I want to watch the matches."

When we get back to the main walkway, volunteers in yellow shirts are posting bracket sheets on the walls. The space fills with kids and parents. Everyone's trying to find their list of matches for the day. Parents take out pens and phones. Kids write match numbers on the palms of their hands. Lev and I stand at the back, craning our necks to see my bracket while Kenna waits for us. We push into the crowd.

"There it is," I say. There are thirteen kids in the U12, 95-pound weight class.

"You've got a tough group. That kid Micah Garvin from the Gold Medal team? I heard he's undefeated."

"Spence is on there too," I say. "You think he'll forfeit today?"

"Actually, he wants to wrestle you. He told me at school."

"You talked to Spence?" I always forget Lev and Nick go to school together.

Lev nods. "His little sister wants to wrestle. Nick's trying to convince their dad it's okay."

"It *is* okay."

"I know that." Lev shrugs. "Don't worry about him. Go out there and wrestle your match."

We stare at each other, then start to laugh again. Lev sounds exactly like Coach Billy. He puts an arm around my neck. "You made it! State championships!" We tie up and grapple in the crowded hallway.

"I'm going to find Isaiah," Lev says. "See you. Nice to meet you, Kenna."

"That's the guy who gave you so much trouble this season? He seems nice," Kenna says, raising her eyebrows at me.

"He turned out to be a really good friend. I wish he were wrestling today."

Lev has changed in the last few weeks. He's not hiding from the noise at the top of the bleachers. His eyes aren't squinting from a headache. I thought coming to States and not wrestling would be hard for him, but Lev seems happy.

"Clear the floor," a voice calls over the loudspeaker. "We're getting ready to wrestle." The whole arena wakes up. Applause and cheers fill my ears.

"I'd better find Coach," I tell Kenna. "Come on. You can sit with my family."

Dad wants to give me a pep talk before I go to the judges' table for my first match. He puts his hands over the cups of my headgear and touches his forehead to mine. "In it to win it?"

"You know it."

I run over to check in. "I'm Mikayla Delgado," I tell the judges.

Then I'm in the middle circle, putting on the green cuff. Our ref smiles at me and my opponent, like he's as excited to be here as we are. His hand swoops up. "Wrestle!"

This kid and I are evenly matched. Every move I try, he

has a counter. Every attack he makes, I block. At the end of the first period, there's no score.

"Red chooses down," the ref calls as we set for second period.

On the whistle, I chop the kid's arm, try to break him down, but he's already starting to stand. I cling to my opponent's back, wrapping both legs around his shins. As I curl my feet around his ankles, he stumbles forward. When he puts his hands down to break our fall, I spin him to his back. The ref signals the takedown, then sprawls on the mat next to us.

"Time!" the ref calls. He touches three fingers to his shoulder, back points for me. I hear cheering in the stands. My whole family is out there, and my two best friends, Kenna and Lev. I've got to do this.

It's my turn as down man. If I keep my base, the other guy can't score. The whistle blows. I feel my opponent spin against my back, looking for a hold. My ankles are tucked too deep for him to get a pick.

"Action!" the ref says. "Let's go, guys. This is your warning." When I don't move fast enough, he calls me for stalling and gives a point to the other guy.

We reset. Every time I try to stand, this kid breaks me down, flat on my stomach. But he never turns me, never gets the score. It's not a thrilling way to end the match, but I win, 3–1. I've won a match at the state championships!

The ref raises my arm. "Nice job," he tells me before I run to shake the opposing coach's hand. "I like seeing girls out here on the mat."

He means well, I guess, but it's States. Can't we focus on the match and not the boy-versus-girl thing?

In the stands, my family is cheering. Not just my family. A whole bunch of Gladiators and their parents shout my name. I hear someone scream, "Pink shoes, can't lose!" Was that Kenna? She waves at me, tilts her head toward Lev, and smiles. I know what that means. She thinks he's a good guy.

Evan and Cody meet me in the bleachers. "Did you hear that?" Evan asks.

"Nobody cheers for *me* like that," Cody says. "Good job, Mickey. You killed it."

My mind's already on the next match, with a kid from the Bulldogs. "What's my number?" I ask Dad.

"You have time. Get a snack. Stay warmed up. Way to go, kiddo." Dad pulls me in for another hug. *This is it,* I tell myself. *This is what I wanted.*

Kenna, Lev, Isaiah, and I check out the concessions. Of course, Lev buys a pack of Twizzlers so we can celebrate my win. Without Josh here, we're not the Fearsome Foursome, but something else. It's always been Kenna and me, and I was fine with that. We've made other friends who've come and gone. I didn't mind as long as we had each other. This year, Kenna has Lalita and the kids she met from the "Thriller" act, and I've got my Gladiators. The two of us are still best friends, but we each have a circle of our own, new people who are important to us.

I win my next match, pin the kid in the second period.

People in the stands go nuts. Haven't they ever seen a girl wrestle before?

"Nice boots!" someone shouts from the bleachers as I walk off the mat. I send them a wave.

I have to wait another twenty-five matches until I'm up again, but I'm rising in the bracket. When new bout sheets are posted, my name has moved closer to the championship round.

I look at the consolation bouts. Nick Spence already lost one today. If I keep winning, I won't have to wrestle him. But this morning's matches took a lot out of me. And just my luck, my next opponent is Micah Garvin, the undefeated kid from Gold Medal.

I tell myself not to think about the fact that he's nationally ranked. Like Lev said, I've got to go out there and wrestle my match, no matter who's across the mat.

CHAPTER 36

Lev

On Saturday morning, when Evan and I walk into Towson University's arena, the outside world stops existing. I'm here for Mickey, one hundred percent.

I've never been to a tournament as a fan before. Today, I get to watch Mickey and Isaiah wrestle without worrying about my own matches.

There are a bunch of Gladiators here, but Devin is the first to say hello. He runs up and pulls on my jacket. He doesn't care that I'm not on his team anymore.

"Hey, Devin." I pick him up and throw him over my shoulder. He's all legs. In a couple of years, he'll be tall like Isaiah. "You ready to kick butt out there?"

"Ready!"

I put him down on the mat. "Show me your stance."

He gets low, with his hands up. His face is all pinched, lips smooshed together, eyes narrow. I take my stance across from Devin and let him get a shot on me. He grabs a single leg and takes me down to the mat.

"Two!" Devin shouts. He jumps up and runs circles around me, holding up two fingers.

I laugh and give him a fist bump. "Way to go, man. I've got to find Mickey. You wrestle hard when it's your turn tomorrow."

Last week, I asked Josh and Isaiah to video chat with me. I explained my idea for helping Mickey, and how I thought it might help Nick too. It was the way people cheered for that girl at the Naval Academy tournament that gave me the idea. Today, we have a stadium full of wrestling fans. If I ask, I know a whole lot of them will cheer for Mickey. And if a whole lot of people make it clear they want her to wrestle, maybe Dr. Spence will give in.

Thanks to Isaiah's mom, all the Gladiators parents know we need a cheering section for Mickey's matches. Especially if she ends up wrestling Spence.

I asked Josh not to tell his uncle the plan. I don't want Coach Billy getting in trouble with the state wrestling association. We didn't tell Mickey or the Delgados, either. She'll wrestle better if she doesn't know what we're doing.

I stay calm, even though the air is buzzing with nervous energy. Wrestlers run around, playing tag between the seats, acting like normal kids, even though they're the best wrestlers in the state.

The first time I see Mickey, she's with that girl she's always telling me about, Kenna. Mickey says they're best friends, so I'm surprised they're total opposites. Mickey's loud and strong, the way she pushes me and her brothers around. Kenna is quiet. I notice the way she watches people. I bet she was a good defensive wrestler.

While Mickey warms up, Kenna and I walk around the arena. I fill her in on the plan.

"I like it," she says. "Even if it doesn't work, Mikayla's going to see how many people are on her side."

"Do you miss wrestling?" I ask.

Kenna looks at the mats, spread across the arena floor. There are people everywhere, in the stands, gathered on the edges of mats. There are judges, referees, coaches, parents. She pulls a brown curl until it's straight, then shakes her head. "No. I miss Mickey. Wrestling rec was fun, but this isn't for me. I'm a backstage kind of person."

"I'm still trying to figure out what kind of person I am."

"The kind who stands up for his partner," she says. "That's good enough for me."

CHAPTER 37

Mikayla

The Gold Medal kid pins me in twenty-three seconds. He crows and stamps his feet. He even flexes his biceps at the bleachers. What a show-off.

My brothers and Lev huddle around me. Cody rubs my upper arms. They're bright red. The Gold Medal guy was squeezing me so hard, there are finger marks on my muscles.

"Are you okay, Mikayla?" Mom examines my arms. "We should take you to see the trainer."

"I'm fine."

Evan says, "Let me handle this, Mom." He leans down and gets in my face, the way Dad does after a tough match. "You made it all the way to the semifinals. Do you know how amazing that is?"

"Why, because I'm a girl?"

I try to walk away from Evan, but Cody catches me. "Don't be an idiot," he says. "You were one match away from winning the whole tournament. Girl or not, that's pretty boss."

"Sorry," I say. I know I'm having an awesome day, but I hate getting beat like that, caught in a pinning combination before I even get a shot in. And that kid was the worst sore winner I have ever seen.

I put on my Delgado shirt over my singlet. When Cody saw it this morning, he complained, "Why don't I get one?" and then asked, "Can I have a T-shirt instead of a tattoo?"

Mom said, "That is an excellent idea."

Dad examines a photo of my bout sheet on his phone. "You drop down to match 858. You don't have long to rest. Eat a little something. Drink some water. Stay warm."

"Do you know who I'm wrestling?"

"They haven't updated the brackets yet. Could be Lewis or Spence."

"I'll warm up with you," Lev says.

"What if it's Nick?" I ask him when we find a space to drill.

Lev sits back on his heels and looks at me. "You want some pointers, just in case? I've wrestled Spence a lot. I know what he's going to throw at you."

"That's not cheating?"

"More like scouting."

We practice blocking and breaking cradles, Nick's signature move, but we don't have much time.

My heart speeds up when I pull my cap over my braids, put on my headgear, and check in with the judges. Nick is talking to his father in their corner. I give Lev one last look. He shoots me a thumbs-up from the stands. Kenna waves.

I run to the center of the mat and put on the green cuff.

There's Nick in his royal-blue Eagles singlet, the one my brothers wore when they were my age.

I close my eyes, try to push down my nerves. If he forfeits, I win this match and move on to the bout for third place. But if he wants to wrestle, I'm ready. I'm a Gladiator.

CHAPTER 38

Lev

Spence is strutting around the arena in his blue Eagles singlet. His little sister is trailing behind him. He must be on babysitting duty. The way he picks her up and piggy-backs her, I don't think he minds.

When we pass, I nod to Nick and he nods back. He doesn't know what I'm planning either. He caught me in the sixth-grade hall yesterday and asked if I'd come up with something.

"Leave it to me," I told him. "You focus on wrestling. Nice hair, by the way."

He'd dyed the tips of his floppy hair Eagles blue.

"Thanks. My sister did it with Kool-Aid for States. My dad hates it." Nick grinned. "I won't forget this."

"She's going to beat you, Spence."

"If she does, it'll be a fair fight."

Part of me hopes Mickey and Spence won't have a match today, because that would make everyone's life easier. But at the same time, I want to see if I can make this plan work.

Isaiah comes to give me the report. He's been spying on Mickey's bracket sheet all day. "We're on," he says. "She's wrestling Spence on mat eight."

I slap his hand. "Get everybody who's not wrestling right now. All the Gladiators. All the parents."

"Hey, Lev," Isaiah says. "This isn't the end, is it? You and me, we're going to hang out when the season's over."

"I hope so," I tell him.

My birthday is in the summer. I've never invited wrestling friends to my party before, but I want Josh, Isaiah, and Mickey, maybe even Devin, to be there. Bryan too, of course. Emma, Marisa. My guest list is going to be huge.

I run into the stands to find my team. After all the years of practices, spending weekends at tournaments together, the Gladiators moms and dads know me. They pat me on the back as I walk down the steps and take a seat next to Kenna and the Delgados.

"This is it," Kenna whispers. "Good luck."

Mickey and Spence are at the judges' table. They stand side by side without looking at each other. Coach Billy is in one corner, clapping his hands together. Dr. Spence is on the other side, standing stiff as a board. Nick's sister sits in the coach's chair. She has a blue streak in her hair like her brother's.

"C'mon, Nicky!" she shouts.

It all plays out in front of me, the way it has so many times this season, but now I see things differently. Nick looks at his father. I can tell, the way his shoulders cave, that he wants his dad to say, *Yes, Nick can wrestle*. He doesn't want to throw away a shot at placing in the state tournament.

Dr. Spence shakes his head, the way he has every time Nick and Mickey stepped on the mat this season.

The ref walks Mickey to the center circle by herself. My heart pounds. Kenna grabs my arm and squeezes.

Before the ref can raise Mickey's hand, I shout, "Let her wrestle!"

A few voices join in, yelling, "Let her wrestle!"

Coach Billy looks into the stands. The ref looks up too. Then Dr. Spence.

"Go, Mickey!" Kenna calls. "You've got this."

Evan turns to me and smiles. He cups his hands around his mouth. "Let her wrestle!" he shouts.

"Let her wrestle!" The Delgados join the rest of the Gladiators parents, picking up the chant. Soon it spreads through the stands, louder and louder, beyond where the Gladiators are sitting. Other people, parents and wrestlers, pick up the words. "Let her wrestle!"

Nick spots me. He tips his head and I nod back. He shoots a glance at his father. Dr. Spence wipes his forehead. It's the first time I've ever seen him look nervous.

The chant gets louder. "Let her wrestle!" People walk over to mat eight, to see what's going on. "Let her wrestle! Let her wrestle!"

It feels like the entire stadium is focused on Mickey, standing alone in the center of the mat.

Nick says something to his father. He points at his sister. Dr. Spence looks down at her and nods. Then Nick is running back to the judges' table. His face is all headgear and smiles as he takes his stance across from Mickey.

Applause and cheering surround me as Mickey and Spence shake hands. Dr. Spence turns his back to the mat. For a second, I think he's going to walk away and make Nick wrestle without a coach. But he gathers Nick's sister up, kneels on the mat with her, and claps his hands together.

Kenna hugs me. "We did it."

"Wrestle!" the ref shouts. Mickey gets the first shot. She goes for a double leg and misses, but recovers quickly. They grapple for most of the first period. Nick tries to turn her. He's got good upper-body strength, but he can't get a grip on Mickey. Seconds before the period ends, she trips him. They're on the ground. Mickey crawls up Nick's body to the top position.

"Two!" the ref calls.

"Woo-hoo, Mickey!" Kenna yells.

Behind us, Isaiah's mom is on her feet, clapping. "That's how we do it!"

The ref flips the disk between periods. When it lands on red, Nick chooses down position. Mickey tries to ride him out, but Nick is too strong. He gets a reversal and cradles her up, exactly like I said he would. She kicks out and gets to her belly, but he still earns two back points before the buzzer. She's losing 4–2.

They set up again. Coach Billy crosses his arms in an X. He wants Mickey to take neutral. She's got to get the first shot, the first takedown, if she's going to tie the score. Nick goes for the double leg, but he's too high. Then they're both on their knees, with Nick's arms clasped behind Mickey's hips, and his head in her belly.

"Get out of that!" Cody yells.

Mickey's left arm pops up to break the hold. She's got him by the shoulder. Her free hand comes across and grabs Nick's hip.

Evan looks back at me. "Cement mixer," he says.

She steps up and shifts her upper body so fast, Nick turns onto his butt and then on his back.

She's already got the takedown, but Mickey's going for a pin. The ref is on his stomach, counting. Nick slips out of the hold, but it's too late. Mickey's got enough back points. He'll need more than an escape to beat her.

The final buzzer sounds. I look up. The ref raises his hand with the green cuff and touches three fingers to his shoulder. The score machine flashes: 4 to 7.

Evan, Cody, Kenna, Isaiah—we're all jumping up and down in the stands like a bunch of kangaroos. Mickey's grin is huge when she goes to shake hands with a red-faced Dr. Spence. Then she leans down and shakes hands with Nick's sister too.

"I'm going to cry," Kenna says.

"Me too," says Cody. I think he's joking.

Mrs. Delgado comes over to me. She has tears in her eyes. "Thank you for being such a good friend to Mikayla." She gives me the kind of hug you only get from a mom.

When Mickey finally makes it into the stands, she faces me with her hands on her hips.

"Your idea?"

I shrug.

She wraps an arm around my shoulders and gives me a noogie. "You're a good partner, Lev Sofer."

"If you say so."

"I say so."

Mickey ends up winning fourth place, good enough for a trophy. It's a boy trophy, of course, which surprises no one. I'm surrounded by a scrum of Delgados. Evan, Cody, and Mickey beg and plead with their mom and dad, insisting that Mickey has earned all the donuts she can eat. Kenna and I look at each other and laugh.

"You'll get used to them," Kenna says. "It's a Delgado thing."

"I know a great donut place five minutes from here," Mr. Delgado says. "You're all coming. My treat."

Before we leave the arena, I look for Spence. If his dad is still busy coaching, he'll be able to talk. Finally, I see Nick and his sister sitting in the upper tier of seats. It's hard to miss their matching blue hair.

Mickey follows my eyes. "I'll go with you," she says. "Can you wait for us, Kenna?"

When we're nearly at the top, Mickey can't help herself. She has to say it, one last time. "Nice view, Sofer."

"Nice view," I agree.

Nick and I clasp hands. "Not what I expected," he says, "but at least we got to wrestle. Good match, Delgado."

Mickey nods. "You too. I hope you get to wrestle some-day, little Spence," she says to Nick's sister. Mickey reaches into her wrestling bag. "Here. They're a little big, and you'd better wash them, but promise me you'll wear these on the mat someday." She hands Nick's sister her pink hedgehog knee socks.

When Nick's sister smiles, I can see she's missing at least four teeth.

"Pink shoes, can't lose," she tells Mickey.

"Was that you cheering for me this morning?" Mickey asks. She grabs the little girl around the neck and ties up with her, grappling right there in the seats.

"We'd better go," I tell Mickey. "Donut time. See you at school, Spence."

"See you, Sofer," he says.

It feels good, sitting with my friends in the donut shop at the end of a long day of wrestling. For once, I'm not in my sweaty singlet, hair crunchy and flattened from wearing headgear all day. Mickey's parents and her brothers sit at the counter. Mickey, Kenna, and I have a booth to ourselves. There's a box of donuts and three big glasses of milk sitting in the middle of the table.

Kenna points to Mickey's trophy. "Did you have to bring that in here?"

"Trophy Boy wants donuts too," Mickey says.

I pick up the trophy. "He's a worthy partner for Trophy Girl. Does Kenna know about the prank?"

Mickey nods. She holds up her glass of milk. "Partners."

Kenna holds up her milk. "And friends."

We clink our glasses together. This is what I'll write about in my notebook tonight, so I'll always remember sitting in a donut shop with my friends, a trophy from States gleaming on the table. Even if I never step on the mat again, this has been my best season.

ACKNOWLEDGMENTS

My son had been wrestling for several years when I began taking my writing notebook to practices and competitions. The sport was such a big part of our family's life, I knew I'd tell a wrestling story someday.

This book would not exist without the support of the wrestling community. Coaches Brian Dykstra and Will Land were mentors during my son's early years in the sport. Thank you to the dedicated parents and coaches of Howard County Vipers Wrestling.

In relearning the rules, vocabulary, and strategies of wrestling, Jay LaValley, 2012–2016 chairman of the Maryland State Wrestling Association (MSWA), was my go-to resource. I value his assistance and his friendship. Jay and Jani Palmer, MSWA Women's Director, 2014–2016, have been instrumental in making the sport available to young athletes of all genders. Author Denise Wilcox and her husband, National Wrestling Hall of Fame coach Steve Wilcox, were kind enough to review my manuscript and make sure I had the wrestling scenes right.

As research for this book, I conducted interviews with athletes, parents, and coaches. Jason Dickson, Tina Gordon, Mary Holmes, Jay LaValley, Jani Palmer, and Tony Patelunas were generous with their time and their stories.

I'm lucky to have a team of friends and critique partners whose feedback I value: Veronica Bartles, Margaret Dilloway, Karina Glaser, Mike Grosso, Jennifer Lewis, Casey Lyall, Joy McCullough, Lee Gjertsen Malone, Ki-Wing

Merlin, Naomi Milliner, Stacey Riedmiller, Amie Rose Rotruck, Shari Schwarz, Michelle Warshauer Smith, and Timanda Wertz. The members of the Sweet 16s author group have been colleagues and champions, especially Melanie Conklin, who always has an encouraging word when I need one, or several. Lev's name was a gift from my aunt, Jonine Sofer.

My editor, Wendy Lamb, and assistant editor, Dana Carey, must have been surprised when I first pitched a wrestling book. I appreciate their faith in me and their help in nurturing Lev and Mikayla's story. Stephen Barbara may not be a wrestler, but he deserves a trophy for Most Encouraging Agent. I am grateful to the wonderful team at Random House Children's Books for their work on *Takedown*.

If being supportive of your spouse were an Olympic event, my husband would have brought home a gold medal long ago. We loved watching our children compete in sports when they were young. Though they've moved on to other interests, I consider Robbie and Julia honorary Gladiators.